I0789483

HELLO MY CHILD

DEVOTIONAL

Cecilia D. Porter

Table of Contents

WAITING ON GOD

HELLO MY CHILD,

I know that you can't understand why it is taking so long for me to answer your prayer. I heard you begging me to help you.

I see your tears. I know that you have a contrite and broken spirit. I feel everything that you are going through. I know that you are fasting and praying.

You think that I am punishing you for something. Maybe, for an unrepented sin. You are trying to figure out how you can expedite your prayer request. I know that you are faithfully fasting and praying, please continue. I am working it out for you. Answers to your prayers are being hindered by unseen forces and obstacles, but they will be answered. They may not be answered when you want them, but I am always on time. I always come through for my children. It may not be what you prefer, but it will always be perfect for you. My timing is always perfect.

Look at it like this, when a woman becomes pregnant, she's expecting a child. The baby has to go through incubation for usually nine months. The baby goes through different stages, as it is formed to what I want it to be. To the average person, that may not be long, but for the one who is caring for the baby, it's a long time.

During the process the baby becomes heavier each month. The closer the due date, the heavier the load. When that expected date is here, before the relief there will be pain. Unexplainable pain. Indescribable pain. Out of the pain, comes the blessing. While you are awaiting an answer to your prayer, you will feel the heaviness of patience. That's right, I am teaching you patience.

You may go through some pain, while you are waiting for me to answer your prayer. That pain will teach you to be patient. Then after the pain, you will receive the blessing of patience.

So my child, please be patient, your prayer request is processing. Just wait on it, I promise you, it will be worth the wait. I have never failed you and I never break my promises.

Your Heavenly Father

WIIFM - WHAT'S IN IT FOR ME?

What's in it for me? Is a question you would ask a person to find out: What would you gain, benefit or profit from an arrangement from participating in something.

WIIFM (What's In It For Me?), whether verbalized, inwardly expressed, or texted, is an expression that has become increasingly popular.

This is a selfish and self-centered attitude, but it is not new. This attitude has been around since the beginning of mankind. It appears that people are so preoccupied with self and this attitude is growing faster than our national debt.

God foretold this self-centeredness as "love of self," as one of the outcomes of a world gone wild. God inspired the Apostle Paul to write to Timothy, "But know this, that in the last days perilous times will come: For men will be lovers of themselves, lovers of money, boasters, proud, unloving, haughty, lovers of pleasures rather than lovers of God". (2 Timothy 3:1-4)

God, our Creator, knew that mankind would be self-absorbed and it would thrive in epidemic proportions. As a Christian, when we look at the question, "WIIFM." Titus 3:3-6 screams out, "At one time we too were foolish, disobedient, deceived and enslaved by all kinds of passions and pleasures. We lived in malice and envy, being hated and hating one another. But when the kindness and love of God our Savior appeared, not because of righteous things we had done, but because of his mercy. He saved us through the washing of rebirth and renewal by the Holy Spirit whom he poured out on us generously through Jesus Christ our Savior, so that, having been justified by his grace, we might become heirs having the hope of eternal life."

As a Christian, being Christ-like, there is no room for MMI, Me, Myself, and I. God expects us to love others as we love ourselves, and love others as Jesus Christ loves us. God expects us to accept His Son, the Lord Jesus, as our Savior. He expects us to give our lives to Him and in so doing, develop the character of Christ. God wants us to become more like Himself.

The question WIIFM, shouldn't exist for a true Christian. The question is always and in every situation should be "What would Jesus do?" Most importantly, we are to serve others. Galatians 5:13

clearly states, "For dear brothers, you have been given freedom: not freedom to do wrong, but freedom to love and serve each other."

What does Jesus want from you? For you to use every opportunity you have to do good for others and to serve them. He tells us that if we do something good to the least of our fellow man, it is as though we have done it to Him, personally.

As humans, we all enjoy the pleasures of life, friends, family, food, nice things, etc. But all of these things will come to an end. Our meals will be over, our jobs will come to an end, parties are short lived, and we all will eventually die. God offers us what we can experience forever, a joyful, meaningful life with Him, forever, in His kingdom.

THAT'S LIFE!

One of the very first lessons we learn as children is that life isn't always fair. Most of us cling to that belief. This belief influences our expectations and can cause us to view the world as a series of transactions: Work hard, you should get a promotion. Treat others with kindness, you should get the same in return.

When there is a gap between what is and what we believe should be, we tend to get angry. "I don't deserve this!" But dwelling on unfairness doesn't actually make life fairer, it does, however, make it difficult to think rationally and keeps us focused on problems instead of solutions. We don't get to choose what happens to us, but we do get to choose how we react to the things that happen to us.

Take the story of Joseph, from prisoner to prince. Joseph was the beloved son of Jacob and Rachel. He was sold by his jealous brothers. He was eventually brought to Egypt, where he was sold to Potiphar, one of King Pharaoh's ministers. Divine success enabled him to find favor in his master's eyes, and he was appointed head of Potiphar's estate. Potiphar's wife turned the tables on Joseph, telling her husband that it was Joseph who had tried to entice her, thus causing Joseph to be thrown in prison. Joseph, while in prison, had the opportunity to interpret King Pharaoh's dreams. Impressed by Joseph's wisdom, Pharaoh appointed him as his viceroy, second only to the King himself, and tasked him with readying the nation for the years of famine.

That's life! Life isn't fair! One minute you are riding high and the next minute you are knocked down. As soon as you get up, you are back down again. Life is at times funny and at times traumatic. As soon as your dreams appear to be materializing, someone comes along and stomps on your dreams.

Wherever God guides you, He will provide for you. God's Word encourages us, in the midst of our trials and our frustrations. We all have dreams for our lives. We plan and work hard, and save, but financial struggles still hit. We have friends and family who we cherish, but relationships still shatter. We love and marry and have children, but families are still torn apart.

Before the world was formed, we were God's children. After we die, we will be God's children. God knows that life has not been fair to us. We, for the most times, didn't do anything wrong. God knows that we are not perfect. He knows there are consequences to our actions. Life begins with our birth and it will end in our death. Our spiritual life begins with Jesus Christ, and after death, is eternal life.

Life isn't fair, this we know. And it would be quite unfair to expect it to be, knowing that God told us that we would face troubles in our lives. Yes, there will always be trouble along the way. Some days, staying strong can be so exhausting that giving up seems like the easiest option. However, what you must always remember is that God also assures us that there will be victory, and He never stops reminding us that we have strength in Him.

"Be strong and courageous. Do not be afraid or terrified because of them, for the Lord your God goes with you; he will never leave you nor forsake you" (Deuteronomy 31:6).

Sanctification means, "to be set apart," for a specific purpose. Sanctification involves separation, dedication, purity, consecration, and service. In being set apart and separate from sin, he or she is separated unto God. By belonging to the family of God, he or she is identified with God and made pure. Being consecrated, he or she is set apart for God's use in acceptable service.

"Now may the God of peace sanctify you completely; and may your whole spirit, soul, and body be preserved blameless at the coming of our Lord Jesus Christ. He who calls you is faithful, who also will do it." 1 Thessalonians 5:23-24

When a person is sanctified he or she is being set apart by God for a specific divine purpose. The very moment we are saved in Christ, we are also immediately sanctified, and begin the process of being conformed to the image of Christ. As children of God, we are "set apart" from that moment, to carry out His divine purpose, unto eternity. Hebrews 10:14 says, "For by one offering He has perfected forever those who are being sanctified."

Even though we have been "set apart," we continue to behave in ways that are contrary to God. Paul tells us that there is an inner battle being waged within us. A battle between our old sinful nature and our new nature. Paul describes the two forces at work within us — the Holy Spirit and our evil inclinations. "For the flesh lusts against the Spirit, and the Spirit against the flesh; and these are contrary to one another so that you do not do the things that you wish." Galatians 5:17

Sanctification is an inward spiritual process where God brings about holiness and change in a Christian by means of the Holy Spirit.

We are all faced with challenging issues. We all have struggled with sin. We all have a past life. We all have done things that were not pleasing to God. But once we accepted Jesus into our lives, the Holy Spirit entered our lives and started a transformation process. The Holy Spirit convicts us on the areas that need changing, to help us grow into holiness.

We will never be without sin, but through God's sanctification, we will sin less. 1 John 1:18, "If we say that we have no sin, we deceive ourselves, and the truth is not in us."

We are a work in progress. Every believer, every day of our lives, we are in the process of sanctification. The process is personal for each of us. No one is on the same level. Our purposeful goal is to be "sinless" because we will not be "sinless" until we are marked present in our heavenly home.

THE GAMES THAT PEOPLE PLAY

When we were kids, we played so many different games. Games like DodgeBall, Freeze, Simon Says, Monopoly, Softball, Hopscotch, Hide and Seek, etc. One of the best things about being a child for me was Christmas, summer, and playing games.

"When I was a child, I spoke as a child, I understood as a child, I thought as a child, but when I became a man, I put away childish things" 1 Corinthians 13:11.

We all grow up, or do we? So why when we grow up, we still want to play games? Playing games really hurts people. People will play games to get something they want. They even play games in their relationship. What do people get out of playing games in relationships? The answer is quite simple, they are getting something out of it.

Unfortunately, people are still playing games. These games hurt people when they are played. They are played to get something that is wanted, to protect themselves from hurt or embarrassment, or for any number of reasons. Even when someone becomes saved and becomes a Christian, the games sometimes continue.

Some people are playing Hide and Seek. In the game of Hide and Seek one hides until he or she is found. The adult version of these games is that they drop out of church for whatever reasons. They don't know that their spiritual growth is being hindered. God has clearly reminded us in His Word, for us to not forsake the assembly of God. Sometimes they get found and come back to the house of God, and sometimes, sadly to say, some stay lost. "Turn my eyes from looking at worthless things, and give me life in your ways" Psalm 119:37.

Some people like to play Simon Says. In Simon Says, someone would do a particular action and the players would do it only if the leader would say, "Simon Says". In the real world, this may be one of the more popular responses to peer pressures. People dress, talk, walk, listen, believe, and live like everyone else. But not as God would want them to live. Maybe in a way, they think they are expected to live. They are just pretenders. Let's put it this way, they are faking their life. It is all about perception. They are even faking being a Christian. "The Lord tests the righteous, but his soul hates the wicked and the one who loves violence" Psalm 101:3.

Some people are playing DodgeBall. DodgeBall is to avoid being hit by the ball. When you are hit by the ball you are called "out". The winner is the one that was not hit by the ball. The grown-up game of DodgeBall is not much different. People will attack you, and as a Christian, you are attacked often. Not by a ball, per se, but those accusations make you feel like you are hit by a ball. That ball that is attacking you comes via vicious accusations, slanderous remarks, deceitful actions, etc. The results, someone is hurt and another person thinks that they are a winner. "An athlete is not crowned unless he competes according to the rules' ' 2 Tim. 2:5.

This world is fleeting and time is running out fast. Sadly to say, some people will spend their entire life playing games. Life is meant to be enjoyed and it's okay to have fun and play fun games. As Christians, our life is meant for discipleship and service. Our life should be full of spiritual devotion and not worldly ambition. Our life should be a whole-hearted Christian commitment and not half-hearted concerns. Our life should be a serious spiritual life, not just playing games on people, and with God.

"I press on toward the goal for the prize of the upward call of God in Christ Jesus" Philippians 3:14.

A LETTER OF RECOMMENDATION

What is a Letter of Recommendation? A Letter of Recommendation is a letter written by someone who can recommend an individual's work or academic qualifications and skills. They discuss the qualities and capabilities that make the candidate a good fit for a given position.

In 2 Corinthians, chapter 3, Paul addresses the Corinthians church. Some false teachers had started carrying forged letters of recommendation to increase their authority. Paul tells them that he doesn't need any such letter from them. He tells them that the only letter he needed was them, themselves. He goes on to say that he can see the change in their hearts and that they are a letter from Jesus Christ.

As Christians we don't need to advertise that we are Christians. We don't need a Letter of Recommendation from each church we are a member of to validate who we are. Our Letter of Recommendation of Jesus, is not written on a letterhead with pen and ink. Our validation is from the Spirit of the Living God, and is in our heart.

When we gave our lives to Christ, the process of conversion wasn't one for which any human minister could take credit for, it was the work of God's Spirit. We did not become believers in Christ by 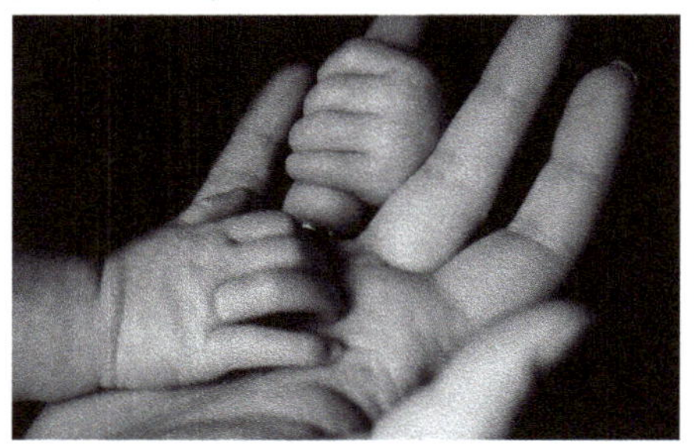 following or using a specific technique. Our conversion was a result of God placing His Spirit in our heart, which caused a Spiritual heart transformation. Can Jesus do it? Oh yes He can!

As Christians, people should know who we are and who we are by our walk. Your walk in Christ is proof and is your Letter of Recommendation. If you want to know if someone's walk with God is authentic, look for these signs: 1) Look for their Motivation, 2) Look for their Patterns, and 3) Look for their "FRUIT".

Motivation: When we are trying to tell if someone is a Christian or not, look for their motivation. You cannot always tell what someone's motive is right away, but give it enough time, and people will show you why they are doing what they are doing.

Pattern: Do they practice what they preach or are they just doing lip service? Do they consistently show the deeds of the "flesh" or show the fruit of the Spirit? Are they living like a person headed to Heaven or like a person headed to Hell?

Their Fruit: There are nine Fruits of the Spirit: love, joy, peace, patience, kindness, goodness, faithfulness, gentleness, and self-control. Usually, when people get in public and around other people, they will act or behave the way they want people to perceive them. Then when they are in private, when no one can see them, they will act just like the person they really are. This fruit shows itself when no one else is looking. It shows itself when we are all alone. This one fruit is "Self-control". Self-control refers to the ability to reject sinful things and to walk away from the deeds of the flesh when you are all alone. It describes the inner constitution that honors God when no one else is looking.

If someone is a child of God, they truly understand that the only way for them to enter Heaven is for God to do everything. There is no place for MMI, that is Me, Myself and I. MMI has no place in the Christian life, because there is no way that you can get credit for your own salvation. God has to call us. God has to justify us. God had to come and die for us. God lives inside of us. God gives us His nature. God gives us His Spirit. It is GOD, GOD, GOD, and God alone.

When we live our lives for Christ, we are a walking Letter of Recommendation.

Merriam Webster dictionary defines "JOY" as the emotion evoked by well-being, success, or good fortune by well-being, of possessing what one desires.

What does the Bible say about joy? "JOY" is a fruit of the Spirit. As the result of being one of the fruits of the Spirit, it is having the indwelling of the Holy Spirit.

You can fake at a lot of things, like faking to be a Christian, but you CANNOT fake joy or having joy. You either have it or you don't. Galatians 5:22-23 states, "But when the Holy Spirit controls our lives he will produce this kind of fruit in us: love, joy, peace, patience, kindness, goodness, faithfulness, gentleness and self-control..."

The Spirit produces character traits, not specific actions. We cannot go out and do the Fruit of the Spirit, and we can't obtain them by trying to get them. If we want the fruit of the Spirit to develop in our lives, we must recognize that all of these characteristics are found in Christ. The way to grow them is to join our lives to His life. We must know him, love him, remember him, and imitate him. The result will be that we will fulfill the intended purpose of loving God.

There is a difference between joy and happiness. Happiness is a pleasure whereas Joy is a sacrifice. Happiness is bliss and Joy is selfless. Happiness is external and Joy is internal. Happiness is an earthly accomplishment and Joy is a spiritual connection with God.

Many people get the two confused. They don't understand the difference between happiness and joy. It is simple, happiness is external and is fleeting. You can be happy one moment and sad the next. Happiness is a feeling brought about through this world. It is a simple pleasure. Whereas, Joy is a spiritual connection with God through Jesus. We can only attain Joy through Christ. Joy is given to us by the Father through the Holy Spirit. Joy is spiritual and it is something that connects us with God, because it is given to us by the Spirit. The Joy in our hearts doesn't think about the pleasures that make us happy, but what is right and moral in the eyes of God.

Simplified: Joy is a spiritual quality that lasts forever. We will always have it. Having joy includes feeling good cheer and having a vibrant happiness. But the spiritual meaning of expressing God's goodness involves more. It is a deep-rooted, inspired happiness. For God's children, the power of joy is never-ending. Although not one fruit of the spirit is more important than another, joy enables us to experience the other fruits in the way that Jesus did.

Happiness is an emotion in which we experience feelings ranging from contentment and satisfaction to bliss and intense pleasure. Happiness is the consequence of a personal effort.

"May the God of hope fill you with all joy and peace as you trust in Him, so that you may overflow with hope by the power of the Holy Spirit" Romans 15:13.

Joy is a deep rooted sense that all things are well, because our God is in charge of all things. We express joy through praise, in songs, and when we laugh. Joy is the peaceful countenance. Joy is the substance of our soul. Joy holds us together in adversity, as we trust God. Jesus wants us to overflow in joy.

In today's time with modern technology, it is easier to send an email than to write a letter. Matter-of-fact, letter writing is a rarity in this Internet age. This world is dominated by texts and email and social media. Holiday cards are replaced by Facebook posts and invitations are received and sent via evite.

For immediate attention or communication, a text or email is the perfect form of communication.

Have you ever received an email that was marked, "Do Not Reply"? A no reply email is an email address that is not monitored and blocks customers from replying.

Sometimes a person or people get so caught up in life and things in this life, that they will have the tendency to "X" everything important out of their lives, including Jesus. Jesus loves us and He will use every method and opportunity to get our attention, to bring things, and Himself back to our remembrance.

Imagine, God sending a wayward child this email, and it's marked

"Do Not Reply":

Hello My Child, if you are receiving this email, that means that you are entering into a reprimand stage and you are beyond excuses.

You see, I made you in my image, not in the image of an animal, or a bird, or a fish, but MY image.

When I made you, I gave you the possessions of rationality, morality, spirituality, and the capacity to relate to ME and with your counterparts.

Your body is for living a meaningful life that glorifies ME as MY image-bearer.

I gave you a body that has a dynamic framework of bone and cartilage that is called a skeleton. Your body has an automatic thermostat that takes care of both your heating and cooling systems, keeping your body temperature at an average of 98.7 F.

I gave you a brain with a complex computer system that computes and sends throughout your body billions of bits of information,

information that controls every action you make, right down to the flicker of your eyelash.

The sounds that you hear in your ear, is being played on a perfect little musical instrument inside of your ear.

Your heart actually is a muscular pump forcing blood through thousands of miles of blood vessels. The blood carries food and oxygen to every part of your body. I gave you your body, in my own image, to glorify ME and to represent ME, and only ME.

When you act-out and show-out, you dishonor ME.

I gave you your hands, to lend a helping hand, not to hurt or destroy. I gave you your ears, to listen to my Word and the cries of others in need, not to entertain unholiness. I gave you a voice to speak my Word, to encourage, and to sing MY praises, not to speak of wickedness. I gave you your eyes, to see the beauty of mankind, to read MY Word, not to explore abomination. I gave you your legs, to walk upright in MY eyes, in the path I chose for you, not for you to deviate from them, not to run toward immorality.

I gave you your heart, to love one another, not to practice and participate in hateful and cruel acts. With that heart of yours, you have broken MY heart.

You should have been thankful for the blessings that I bestowed upon you, but you are not. You should have been thankful for the doors that I opened for you, but you are not. You should have been thankful for the food that I provided for you; for your clothing, your shoes, and the roof that I gave to you, but you are not. You should have been thankful for every mountain that I brought you over and every trial that I saw you through, but you are not.

You are the most ungrateful creation that I created. I just wanted you to know, that you are completely unappreciative of ME and what I have done for you. I don't need for you to provide me with any more unsubstantiated excuses.

PLEASE, "DO NOT REPLY"!

ISOLATION

The definition of isolation is the state of being alone or away from others. Quarantine, alienation, detachment, anomie, estrangement, insulation, secrecy, insularity, solitude, loneliness, purdah, privateness, insularism are others words for Isolation.

Social Isolation is a state of complete or near-complete lack of contact between an individual and society. It differs from loneliness, which reflects temporary and involuntary lack of contact with other humans in the world.

In the future, when we hear the word, "Isolation," we will probably immediately think, "Covid-19". And we will have a lot of stories to share. Not just stories, but "TESTIMONIES". For some, being in "isolation" has been a nightmare. To others, it could be bittersweet. With me, thus far, it has been "bittersweet".

If there was an emotional scale to gage my emotions, my emotions would have hit each digital base all over the board on the chart. My emotions have created its own dance and created its own music and it is a collage of a mixture that is uniquely blended and cannot be replicated and has created an element that is bouncing off of the "Periodic Table" with a symbol that the best scientists cannot decipher.

But yet, being in Isolation isn't all bad. I did say it has been bitter and yet sweet, thus bittersweet. Isolation! Social Distance! Self-Isolation! Quarantine! We all are facing a new normal. Being isolated isn't something that isn't a new thing. The Bible gives us scriptures that tell us about "isolation".

It appears "Isolation" is a necessary requirement for some. It is necessary to complete our Spiritual Journey. Joseph served in the wilderness (isolation), while he was in slavery and in prison, before God used him. Joseph had to wear the chains around his ankles before he could wear the gold chains around his neck. Elijah and Paul, both spent time in the wilderness (isolation), before God sent them out to do His will. Even Jesus had his wilderness (isolation) moments. After John the Baptist baptized Jesus, Jesus was led into the wilderness. He fasted for 40 days and 40 nights and was tempted by The Tempter, himself. Afterwards, Jesus began His public ministry.

So we are in "Isolation". We are having a wilderness experience. But in this wilderness moment, let's thirst for Christ. Let's not be or get angry. Let's not be in despair. Of course, we all are human and we are seeing and hearing things to cause anger and despair. Let us hunger for the Word of God. Let us thirst for Jesus. God got you!!! When this is all over, we should be transformed, new and improved.

While in "isolation" we should have a spiritual growth and a greater intimacy with the Lord. We should be seeking, listening, and praying to God. God is molding us during this time in our lives. We should be drawing closer to Him.

Oh yes, we are in the wilderness as we continue to shelter in place. We are having to be in quarantine. We are in "isolation", but not isolated from God. But afterwards, you should share your wilderness/isolation experience and you should tell your story with boldness. Oh, what a story to tell! Share your testimony of how God brought you over.

My testimony is so "AWESOME"! I can't wait to share it. It is a story that is SO unbelievable, because only God could have made it happen. It all happened while I was in "Isolation," in the wilderness. My story is a testimony and God is still writing it. HALLELUJAH!!!!

I, ME AND MINE

God says that "I" am the great I AM. If you trust "ME", then "I" will do this for you. You are "MINE", "I" am He that can specialize in the impossible.

Our lives should always be about God. When we read His Word, the Almighty God is speaking to us. He points His finger at everything that may cause us problems, disturb our peace, and makes us cry. He knows who our enemies are.

Israel had many enemies and one of their enemies was a small nation called Edom. There was a fortified city in the nation of Edom called Petra. Petra was built into the towering rock southeast of the Dead Sea. When Rev. Porter and I traveled to Israel, we marveled at the sight of this ancient city. It was something to behold, even in its existing condition. Tourists today still marvel at the sight of this ancient Edomite City. So you would wonder how such a remote fortified city could have ever been conquered. But it was conquered, because God had his hand in it. Everything is in God's hands and God can touch whatever He wants.

It doesn't matter what problems you may be facing, God can control them all. There is nothing too hard for God.

Whatever is disturbing your peace, whatever problems that you are faced with, give it to Jesus. The God who uses the first person pronoun of "I, ME, and MINE" throughout the entire Bible, controls all things. "I am the good Shepherd, and know my sheep, and I am known for mine." (John 10:14-15)

Point to each of your problems and let God put His finger on each one. God is trying to tell you, "You are MINE!" "I am in charge!" And, "It will be "ME" that will bring you out!"

God who is The Conqueror, was conquering then and is conqueror now, and will forever more be conquering. How can anyone conquer that which cannot be conquered. God can't be conquered. He is The Conqueror who does the conquering.

John 17:10 says, "All I have is Yours, and all You have is MINE; and in them I have been glorified."

WHO ARE YOU REPRESENTING?

What does it mean to represent something or someone?

To represent means to act or speak officially for someone or something.

When I was young and living at home with my mother, she would always remind us that when we leave home, don't forget, not to embarrass her. As a young girl, I didn't quite know what that entailed. I just knew that I was not going to do anything that would make my mother angry enough to punish me. No way and no how!

My mother had a quiet spirit. She had this rule, you would receive two warnings before you received the physical punishment. The first warning came with a gentle reprimand. The second warning came with a very stern facial expression, with her eyes rolling at you. The third warning, "no reprimand", just the outright, Lord have mercy, physical abuse, and at that time it was called an a#*whipping. In those days it was an outright beat-down. If you do something like that today, it would be considered child abuse, and with time to serve.

As children of God, we are always representing God. To act-out means that you have just embarrassed God. The enemy is always looking at what button they can push on us. Our faith, and our God like character, are always being tested. We will be attacked, talked about, and lied on, because we are targets and the enemy takes target practice, on us, daily. Does he hit the "bullseye" sometimes?

Absolutely! We are God's children and we are Satan's targets. Satan knows our weaknesses and our strengths. He focuses on the weaknesses and keep putting his finger in that sensitive spot, over and over again. Aggravating us, annoying us, disabling us, and trying to hurt us. He knows our pasts, but not our future. So he reminds us of our past over and over again, trying to cripple us. Everyday, he reminds us of our weaknesses. He is constantly nagging us about our past, our mistakes, and our failures. He reminds us that our report card is full of N. F. I. (need for improvement) and tells us, that's unacceptable to God.

We should always remember who we are in Christ. Yes, we all have sinned and come short of the glory of God. We all have a past. A past full of mistakes, shame, guilt, and failures. Yes, we do have a lot of N. F. I. (need for improvement), on our report card of life. The one thing that we need to remember, people are always watching and observing us, and so is God. They can't wait for that flip-side to surface, that old sinful nature that is asleep and not dead. I wish I can say that it's dead for me, but I am going to have to keep it, as the young people say, "one hundred", because, Satan knows that one person, who can push that right button, that can set you off (you know who that person is), and that person can make that old-self, rise and come alive. Then, they will all be looking and saying, "See, I told you that they haven't changed; they are the same old person." In that instance, we forgot who we were representing. People will always remember the bad things that we do, they somehow, never seem to remember the good things that we have done. I wonder, why is that?

God understands our dilemma, and that's why He loves to remind us, that he loves us, and that He has already paid the price for whatever sins we commit, and mistakes we make. He also reminds us that we are always to represent Him. Paul tells us that we represent Jesus: "I therefore, the prisoner of the Lord, beseech you to walk worthy of the calling with which you were called" (Ephesians 4:1). We are no longer darkness, but are light in Jesus. We should walk as children of the light in this world. He has called us. He has chosen us. We are now saints, servants, stewards, and soldiers. We are now witnesses and workers of Christ. Through Jesus, we are victorious, and we have a glorious future. We are ambassadors for God's Son, Jesus. Let's not forget that we represent God!

WHO ARE YOU REPRESENTING?

GENERATION TO GENERATION

Like Advertisers are targeting every imaginable age division, so are the Churches these days are trying to reach every imaginable age group. From the Silent Generation who are also known as the Builders, to the Busters aka Generation X, to Boomers aka Millennials and Generation Y.

From the Builders Generation who literally and metaphorically built this nation after the austerity years post depression and World War 2, to the Baby Boomers who redefined the cultural landscape, to Generation X, who ushered in new technologies and work styles, and now to Generations Y and Z who in this 21st Century are redefining life stages and lifestyles.

We have gone from radio to black and white TV, to color TV, now to internet TV. From long-term savers to lifestyle debt. Psalm 145:4 says, "One generation shall praise Your works to another, And shall declare Your mighty acts." It is the Biblical duty of every generation of Christians, to see to it that the next generation hears about the mighty acts of God. God does not drop down a new Bible from heaven on each generation. He intends for us, the older generation, to teach the new generation about God. He wants the new generation to read and think about him. He wants them to trust and obey Him. He wants them to rejoice over Him and about Him. He wants a true personal relationship from each new generation. Remember the Spirit of God comes down vertically and the truth of God is imparted horizontally.

We must educate our children and grandchildren about God. When we do not introduce our children and grandchildren to God, they will become unemotional, and indifferent about Him. Thus, look at the state of the world today. Anything goes and the Spirit of Morality is dissipating. Our young people would rather be in a club than in church.

The bible says, "Train up a child in the way he should go; even when he is old he will not depart from it." How do we impress faith on our children? It starts with you; and your love for God. It starts in your home and not at church. What's going to impress your children is how you live your life, and your relationship with God. You must talk about Him in your home, in your car, when you lie down and when you get up. The home is the primary place where faith begins, lives, is expressed, and nurtured. The church just reinforced the relationship. Faith is not something that is outsourced, it is a relationship with Christ that must be lived-out.

In the Bible, each generation told the stories of how God brought them over. If our older generation celebrated God's fame and goodness toward them, and He has allowed us to strive in His goodness, then what was true back then, is still true today. God never changes, styles change, time changes, people change, but God will always be the same. We can't live without Jesus, and neither can our future generation.

ON CALL

What is the meaning of "on-call"? Essentially, being "on-call" means that someone is available at a moment's notice. Available at any time and on short notice. "When he calls out to Me, I will answer him; I will be with him in trouble. I will deliver him and honor him" (Psalm 91;15).

Psalm 91 is one of my favorite Psalms. It is my go to scripture when I need Jesus to hear my cries and feel my pain. It is one of my M and M scriptures, meditate and memorize.

These are very sobering times that we are living in. Many people are suffering. They have lost their jobs. The unemployment rate is soaring, the stock market is highly volatile and this Pandemic-Covid-19 is rapidly spreading around the world, like a wildfire. We are in the heat of battle. Troubles are bearing down hard on us and it's heavy. We are feeling the pressures of stress.

People are losing their homes and those that are renting are being evicted in rapid numbers. There are severe floods, fires, hurricanes, hunger, injustice, and people are being mentally affected with all of this turmoil. WE are calling on God like never before, I know that I am, and you are too.

So I am calling unto my heavenly Father, begging Him to send help for me and the world. Then I recite Psalm 91 and I feel comforted as my tears are flowing.

In Psalm 91, God promises: 1) "I will rescue him," 2) "I will protect him," 3) "I will answer him," 4) "I will be with him in trouble," and 5) "I will deliver him". His promises reminds me that we are not alone. God never said that we wouldn't have hard or difficult times. He did say that He would be with us when we face hard times.

Only Jesus can give us rest, peace, and calm. So please don't doubt him. God is always "on-call" and always just "one-call" away. JUST ONE CALL AND THAT'S ALL!

THE GOLDEN RULE

The Golden Rule, is not to be confused with Golden Law, Golden Ratio, or Golden Act. The Golden Rule is the principle of treating others as you want to be treated.

One of Jesus' most famous teachings, the Golden Rule, can be found in the Bible, "So in everything, do to others what you would have them do to you, for this sums up the Law and the Prophets" (Matthew 7:12).

In Luke it reads, "Do to others as you would have them do to you" (Luke 6:31). This is an ethical treatment of others and it is profound and has resonated through the ages. This rule is simple and yet powerful. Simply put, treat people the way that you want to be treated. If you want kindness, give kindness. If you want to be loved, give love. This is a virtue. Virtues are attitudes , dispositions, or character traits that enable us to be and to act in ways that develop our Christlike potential. They enable us to pursue the ideals we have adopted. Honesty, courage, compassion, generosity, fidelity, integrity, fairness, self-control, and prudence are all examples of virtues.

Jesus instructs us to put ourselves in our neighbor's place and guide our behavior accordingly. When we put ourselves in their place, we should be wise enough not to make foolish and evil wishes and desires against them. The Golden Rule displays empathy and reciprocity of morality.

Unfortunately, people don't always treat you the way they want to be treated, nor the way you want to be treated. But that doesn't mean that you don't do the right thing. Two wrongs do not make a right and vengeance belongs to God.

Jesus tells us to "love others," and when we truly "love others" we are simply being obedient to God. God is expecting us to live at peace and in harmony with others; be patient with people; don't judge others; accept people as the person made in God's image; encourage them; serve them; and most importantly, may your acts of love point them to Christ's ultimate love for them.

GOD'S WORD

There is something magical and wonderful found in the falling of snowflakes and raindrops. My grandson loves to feel the raindrops falling on his face. When it happens, he giggles with pure delight. Watching him in the moment, brings a smile to my face and joy to my heart.

You know what else brings a smile to my face and put joy in my heart? Reading God's Word, the Bible! There are different versions of the Bible, but they all are still the Word of God. There are different translations, all with the same message from the manuscripts.

I read the Bible daily, and I have four translations that I will reference, depending on the Scripture. I read the TLB (The Living Bible), NIV (New International Version), the KJV (King James Version), and NLT (New Living Translation) They tell the same message, but in a way that is easy for me to understand.

The message of the Bible is the same in whatever translation I use. The only difference is, there are different means of communicating that message. This is why that there are different translations to cater to everyone. Bible. com says that there are over 2,110 Bible versions in 1,442 languages.

Regardless of how many versions of the Bible there are, if you don't stop to really read God's Word, you will miss the powerful, fulfilling, and rich blessings behind them. The Bible maybe displayed in various forms and places throughout our homes and churches, but if you don't consume His Word, you are missing out of some blessed benefits.

We receive our revelation through the Bible. This is where we need to go, to discover who God is and why we were created. We need the Word of God to help us know what is good and true because it doesn't come to us naturally, "For my thoughts are not your thoughts, neither are your ways my ways, declares the Lord" (Isaiah 55:8).

You need to read the Bible to experience change and growth. You simply can't experience spiritual growth on your own. "All Scripture is breathed out by God and profitable for teaching, for reproof, for correction, and for training in righteousness, that the man of God may be competent, equipped for every good work" (2 Timothy 3:16-17).

The Bible is inspired by God Himself. It is His Word, containing His Wisdom, His Goodness, His Intentions, His Judgements, His Heart, His Promises, His Guidelines, His Instructions, His Truth, His Power, His Comfort, His Encouragement, and His Authority.

The Bible is not simply words about God, it is the Word of God. The Word of God is the VOICE of God in printed form.

I have been studying Romans 5:1-5. I have been meditating on verses 3 and 4, "And not only that, but we also glory in tribulation, knowing that tribulation produces perseverance; and perseverance, character, and character hope." This morning, and for the past few mornings, I woke up thanking God for "HOPE".

Hope is a feeling of expectation and desire for a certain thing to happen. We all are hoping for something and without hope the people will perish. What does HOPE mean in the Bible? "HOPE" is the confident expectation of what God has promised and its strength is in His faithfulness.

Hope is like the light at the end of the tunnel. Hope is a gift from God to encourage us in times when we are feeling down. To have hope is to want an outcome that makes our life better in some way.

It not only can help make a tough situation more bearable, but also can eventually improve our lives, because envisioning a better future motivates you to take the steps to make it happen.

Hope, is looking on the bright side and seeing challenges as opportunities. In other words, "hoping for the best". Hope is a desire for things to change for the better and to want that better situation very much. "Now may the God of hope fill you with all joy and peace in believing, that you may abound in hope by the power of the Holy Spirit" (Romans 15:13).

Hope gives you a vision of what can or will happen. Whether it happens or not, just envisioning it can make you feel better. It can help motivate you to take whatever steps you need to take. Ask yourself, what is it that you are hoping for? If you say "nothing," Houston, we have a problem."

To hope is very important, because "HOPE," is having a light while you are in darkness. This light is Jesus, who helps reveal the path ahead, to show you the way out.

God knows our beginning and ending. What is impossible to man is possible to God. Hope isn't faith. It is not hope that makes things happen, it is faith. God's Word tells us, let the confessions of your mouth be pleasing to God. We know that faith pleases God, and without faith it is impossible to please God. It is important to spend time in the Word, because "faith" comes by hearing and hearing the Word of God.

Things that we are hoping for doesn't always happen immediately and sometimes we just don't understand that we are on a road that is full of road blocks and obstacles. We need faith, bravery, steadfastness, and tenacity to help us persevere toward our vision and goals. Being grounded in the Word of God is the pillar of our strength.

Never lose your hope. It is hope that sustains hope, and hope that will bring us through. Keep your eyes on the prize, and your faith will become unshakeable.

LET'S KEEP "HOPE" ALIVE!

FORGETFULNESS

We forget all kinds of things. The other day, I forgot that I was sauteing some spinach on top of the stove and the burning smell from the spinach brought it back to my remembrance. While driving, we may forget to use our turn signal before we change lanes. We may forget how long the chicken has been in the oven, because we forgot to set the timer. Some people have forgotten how to say, "Please" and "Thank you". They just don't say it to anyone and they don't say it to God. They don't respect God for His many blessings.

Now I can understand if you have a medical condition, perhaps a stroke, Traumatic Brain Injury, Alzheimer's, Dementia, concussion or old-age, for your forgetfulness, but these would be the only legitimate and acceptable reasons to be forgetful about the blessings of God.

There appear to be a universal forgetfulness that is much more premeditated or randomly and systematically, or maybe formally and informally, but how can you forget the goodness of God and about God.

God delivered the Israelites from Egypt. Before they were delivered, they personally saw the power of God through Moses. Moses confronted the most powerful man on earth saying, "Let my people go." Ten plagues later, Moses lead the Israelites out of Egypt with the Egyptian army in hot pursuit. Miraculously, the red sea opens, the Israelites crossed over, and Pharaoh's army is drowned.

Again and again God worked miracles for His people and again and again, and they forgot about God. It almost as though they developed amnesia.

Forgetfulness brings disaster. When people forget God's "many acts of kindness," they will drift away. How easy it is for people to forget God. They turned quickly to the idols around them, money success, the pleasures of the world. We must be very careful not to follow the examples of the Israelites. "They forgot God, their Savior, who had done such great things in Egypt. Such wonderful things in that land, such deeds at the red sea" Psalm 106:21-22.

Forgetfulness is deadly. That is why God's Word gives so much emphasis to calling us to remember. Moses' message to the Israelites in Deuteronomy is warning them not to forget the Lord. This same message is throughout the Bible. Peter tells us to "add to your faith virtue, to virtue knowledge, to knowledge self-control, to self-control perseverance, to perseverance godliness, to godliness brotherly kindness, and to brotherly kindness love. Then he says, "He who lacks these things is shortsighted, even to blindness, and has forgotten that he was cleansed from his old sins" (2 Peter 1:5-9).

We have been rescued from the wrath of God and granted eternal salvation, so how could we ever forget the One who bought us at such a great price. Yet sadly, some people do forget.

Some forgetfulness is not bad. There are somethings that we should forget. Like sins that have been confessed and forgiven. Some past failures that we just keep holding onto. Some mistakes that have been learning experiences. Some bad jokes that don't need to be told anymore.

How can we forget what it cost our Savior to redeem us? How can we forget the greatness of His worth? How can we forget that God in Christ has forgiven us? How can we forget that Jesus has risen from the dead and has conquered every one of our enemies and has given us a sure future in heaven?

Let's not develop a mindset of "Forgetfulness", when it comes to our Lord and Savior, Jesus.

THE PROMPTER

The definition of a "prompter" is a person or thing that prompts. In a theatre, it is a person who prompts or cries out when someone forgets their lines.

Being a Christian is not easy. We are human and the human side is always at battle with the spiritual side. Even after we become a Christian, we still have that sin nature and it declares war on the Holy Spirit. The doxology of Jude 1:24-25 says, "Now to Him who is able to keep you from stumbling and to present you faultless before the presence of His glory with exceeding joy. To God our Savior, who alone is wise, be glory and majesty, dominion and power, both now and forever. Amen."

The audience to whom Jude wrote was susceptible to heresies and to temptations toward immoral living. He encouraged the believers to remain firm in their faith and trust in God's promises for their future. This was important because they were living in a time of increased apostasy. We too, are living in the last days, much closer to the end than we think. We too, are tempted to give in to sin.

We are to keep ourselves in God's love. God is the one that keeps us. Our righteousness does not come from ourselves, but from God. Our security comes from God, who is our Protector. We can only rely on His power, not our own.

We must train our ears to tuned into the insistent voice of God, and heed to His whispers, and obey His Word. Just like the "prompter" that assist those on the theatre stage, and those tele-prompters that assist the newscasters on television, Je-sus is our "Prompter". His eyes are on our script that He has written for us. He simply reminds us of His Words, for us to stay on track, on point, and on His script. When we fall down, stumble, or trip, He helps us to get up, because He is still "prompting" us. The "Prompter", is quick and prompt to help us say the right things, and do the right things, at the right time. We just need to pay attention to the "Prompter," who is Jesus.

The only wise God, is able to keep us from falling. Literally, "He keeps us from falling. He is able to present us faultless before the presence of his glory with exceeding joy."

Our Savior, Jesus Christ, is able to keep us from the errors of our ways. Jesus is the "Prompter," we can trust that He is faithful, and able to keep His grip on us, by prompting us. Only with His help, can we live a holy life that God desires for us to live.

THE TRUTH AND NOTHING BUT

John 14:6 says, "Jesus said to him, 'I am the way, and the truth, and the life. No one comes to the father except through me."

The "Truth"! I promise to tell the truth and nothing but the truth so help me, God. That is the sworn testimony that is given by a witness in court, raising their right hand, with their left hand resting on the Holy Bible.

The oath: Do you solemnly swear that you will tell the truth, the whole truth, and nothing but the truth, so help you God? If not the truth be told, they will be charged with the crime of perjury.

But what do you do when you are surrounded by lies and liars? There are people who are compulsive liars. You can ask a person the most innocent of questions, and what will you receive, a lie in response.

You don't even have to open your mouth to deceive people, just don't tell them what you don't want them to know. The enemy is full of lies and so are his soldiers.

Those who lie, twist life so that it looks attractive and powerful. Lies don't do anything but hurt and is deceitful. They don't have any true power, except the false sense of power to the liar. Lies don't help anything, fix anything, or cure anything. Lies destroy one's character, not develop it. It wounds the mind, the heart, the spirit, and the soul.

Jesus is the "Truth'! You don't have to listen to lies and you must not believe the lies nor the liars. So what do you do? Turn to God and to God's Word. God's Word is the "Truth". The "Truth," you must read it. You must think it. You must pray it. You must declare it.

Christ Jesus said, "Ye shall know the truth, and the truth will set you free" (John 8:32). That is a wonderful promise that can be taken seriously and can never be broken. You can find encouragement, joy, peace, healing, and strength in God's never changing "Truth".

Regardless of what's troubling you, be it a difficulty, illness, financial hardship, a troubled relationship, or anything else, consolation can be found in the Word of God, "The Truth".

THE CARNAL CHRISITIAN

What is a "carnal" Christian? Well, let's define the word, "carnal". Carnal is translated from the Greek word sarkikos, which literally means, "fleshy". The dictionary defines carnal as pertaining to or characterized by the flesh or the body, its passions and appetites.

What is a Christian? A Christian is a person who believes in Jesus Christ and follows his teachings.

Is there such a thing as a "Carnal Christian"? YES! Paul says, "And I, brethren, could not speak unto you as unto spiritual, but as unto carnal, even as unto babes in Christ" 1 Corinthians 3:1.

To live carnally, satisfies the flesh rather than pleasing and honoring God. A carnal Christian may have accepted the gift of salvation, but not the sanctifying work of the Holy Spirit, and the transforming power of the inner man.

All of us Christians, are still works in progress. We still have some areas in our lives where we may at times live carnally, because we are not perfect, yet.

A Carnal Christian, is not willing to "present his or her body as a living sacrifice pleasing and acceptable to the Father" (Romans 12:2).

The Carnal Christian, lives in the lust of the flesh, the lust of the eyes, and the pride of life. Simply put, they are fleshy minded. Paul says that they are babes in Christ. They are unable to digest solid spiritual food, and they are filled with strife, envy, and division. As I said earlier, we were all carnally minded at one time or another, but we have matured in Christ. We are supposed to grow up and become mature. This is a process that continues daily.

It is God's will for a Carnal Christian, to mature and grow from milk to solid food. This is done through faith and a walk of obedience.

But you can overcome the works of the flesh. How? Through the Spirit of God, and by renewing of your mind. "Do not be conformed to this world, but be transformed by the renewing of your mind, that you may prove what is that good and acceptable and perfect will of God" (Romans 12:2).

Renewing your mind, can be initiated at any time with the help of the Holy Spirit, who is living within you. When we have the mind of Jesus, and the Holy Spirit in us, then we have options to be spiritually minded, and we will start thinking like Jesus. God can renew your mind, and refocus your thoughts.

What is "Honesty"? Most people think that "honesty" means that you "don't tell someone a lie" and that speaking the truth is being "honest". Honesty is much more than that. Honesty extends to your actions and the motive behind your actions. If you hide what you did because you were trying to trick someone, that isn't being honest. That's not being honest with yourself, others, nor God.

The adjective, honest is perfect for describing someone who tells the truth. If you are always honest, it means you are truthful and sincere no matter what. The noun honest is the quality of being honest.

Honesty is a facet of moral character that connotes positive and virtuous attributes, such as integrity, truthfulness, straightforwardness, including straightforwardness of conduct. Along with the absence of lying, cheating, theft, etc. Honesty also involves being trustworthy, loyal, fair, and sincere.

What does the Bible say about honesty? Proverbs 12:22 says, "Lying lips are an abomination to the Lord, but those who act faithfully are His delight."

Honesty is truthfulness. An honest person has the habit of making accurate, trustworthy statements about life, self, others, and God.

Honesty! God expects and deserves honesty. It has been said that honesty is the best policy. What is important to know is, honesty is God's policy.

Sometimes it isn't easy trying to be honest. Sometimes it is tempting to lie, misrepresent a situation or ourselves, or downplay the truth. Sometimes being honest is painful. Sometimes being honest is uncomfortable. Sometimes being honest will hurt other people's feelings.

Honesty is next to Godliness. If you want to live a life of Godly integrity, look no further, the best examples of integrity is found in God. God is the foundation of integrity. God is who He is. He told Moses, "I AM WHO I AM", in Exodus 3:14. God is who He is and He never changes. He is blameless and eternally the same. He is perfect and just. He is the God of truth. He is righteous and upright.

So in being a person of Integrity, you always want to be honest with others, yourself, and with God. You always want to be truthful, because it will be God that holds us accountable for everything that we do. We can never be dishonest and think that God doesn't know about it. God sees all and knows all, and nothing ever escapes Him.

Remember, "Honesty" is not only the best policy, it is the only policy because it is God's policy.

PROMISES, PROMISES, PROMISES

People always make promises, but most of them are never honored. Promises, promises, promises! Life is full of people making promises. Politicians are notorious for making promises. Once they are elected, they develop amnesia.

Promises, promises, promises! Promises are made at weddings. "I, take thee to be my wife/husband, to have and to hold, from this day forward; for better, for worse, for richer, for poorer, in sickness and in health, to love and to cherish, till death do us part." So why when times get tough, we break our vows? So why, as of today, 39% of marriages in the US are ending in divorce?

Some people use the word "promise" like a promise is nothing more than a good intention that is easily discarded. There is a old cliche' that says, "promises are made to be broken". Remember, I did say it was an old cliche' and I am not in agreement with this cliche'. A promise, is a promise, and promises are not meant to be broken.

There is ONE who will make us a promise and it will never be broken. God will never break a promise. Jesus is "The Promise Keeper!" When God makes a promise, it is absolutely trustworthy.

In the Bible, the Old Testament promises us a Messiah and in the New Testament, we receive God's promises of the Messiah and God's guidance through the Holy Spirit.

God is always faithful and He is faithful to us in His promises. "God is not man, that he should lie, or a son of man that he should change his mind. Has he said, and will he not do it? One has he spoken, and will he not fulfill it?" (Numbers 23:19)

God is our Creator and the Lord over all of our lives. His nature is good, merciful, and He is true to His word. God promises reflects His qualities. What He promises, He will deliver.

The Bible is the source of truth and God is faithful to fulfill all of His promises. As you read the Bible about the promises of God, claim them.

Whatever your needs are, give them to God. You need a financial blessing, take it to God. You feel lost, take it to God. If you are hurting, take it to God. If you are feeling depressed, take it to God.

God also gives us an unconditional promise. An unconditional promises is simply one in which God says he will do something, and nothing we can do will stop it from happening. Unconditional promises do not depend on the actions of us, only God. Even if we are unfaithful, God will always be faithful to His Word.

God is a promise keeper, He will never renege on a promise.

"Now thanks be unto God, which always causeth us to triumph in Christ and maketh manifest the savior of his Knowledge by us in every place." 2 Corinthians 2:14

"Always" is defined as: at all times; on all occasions. God is our never ending source of support and comfort. A source that we cannot live without. A source that will "always" be there at our time of need. The Bible tells us, and reminds us of what promises God has made to us when it comes to Him. He promised us that He will "always" be present in our lives.

When we are weary and call upon Him, He will give us strength. When we grieve, God will wipe away all of our tears. When we are weary, God will give us strength to carry on.

Whatever we are faced with, God will be our Provider and Protector. Whatever we may have to endure, God will be our Sustainer. We can "always" rely on God to provide us with our resources because He is our Source. God will hold our hands and take us through every situation while we are living our life. There is no circumstance that is too hard for our God.

God has promised us that He will "ALWAYS" come to our aid when we need Him. You know what? He can't lie! God "always" rescues us. He is "always" on time. He may not show up when we want Him to, but His timing is not our timing and His timing is timed perfectly. What you need to know is that God is faithful and He will faithfully come to our aid when we call Him. "ALWAYS!"

"...And lo, I am with you always even to the end of the age." (Matthew 28:20b)

No matter what we are going through, God will "always" be there with us, no matter how long the wait, for Him to answer our prayers.

What God starts, He will finished, you better believe that!

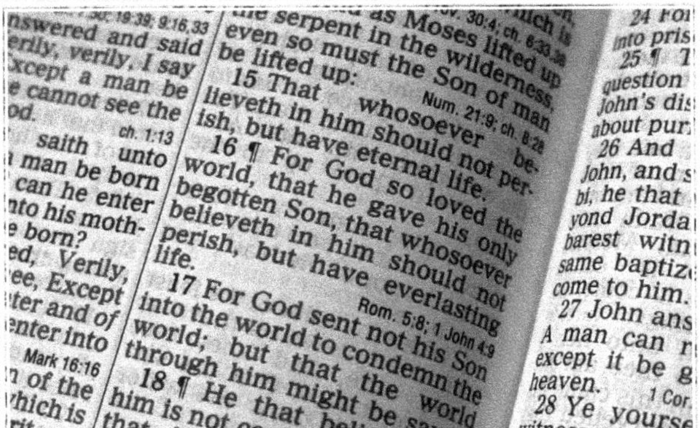

LET ME LOVE YOU

HELLO MY CHILD,

LET ME LOVE YOU

I see that have had a very painful break-up. You are truly going through a very painful experience. I am so sorry. I know that it is painful. I know that you are hurting. You think that nobody understands the pain that you are going through. That nobody really, truly understands. I understand. I understand very well, better than you really know. I know that breakups sucks and that they are the worst.

You feel that your heart has been broken. You have what they say is the Broken Heart Syndrome. You have headaches, because your brain thinks that you are physically hurt. Also, because your heart is broken, one or two things will probably happen, you are either going to binge eat or eat nothing. You will either lose weight or gain weight. You are going through a traumatic experience, your self-esteem level will drop and I know that you are going to get depressed and have some anxiety. I know that you are going to withdraw.

Love is as addicting as drugs. Your body is going to go through withdrawal, because love is addicting and now you think that you are without it. You are thinking that no one loves you. But the Good News is that you are LOVED. I LOVE YOU and I always have and always will. You haven't stopped loving me, but you placed me second and I can never be anything but first place. I have always loved you. Let me love you. Let me in. I have loved you since before you were born and can't nothing keep me from loving you. For Paul has told you "who shall separate us from the

love of Christ? Shall trouble or hardship or persecution or famine or nakedness or danger or sword?" (Romans 8:35)

I know it will take time for your heart to heal, but it will heal. Just lean on me for help. Put me first in your life and I will send the perfect mate for you. The one that I have designed for you. In the meantime, just concentrate on me and let ME love you.

It's just you and me, and it's just the way I like it.

XOXO (hugs and kisses), Love God

FIGHTING DRAGONS

DRAGONS! Our lives are full of dragons. What dragons? The sum of our fears and the heaviness from our burdens. We are always fighting dragons, on the daily. The enemy is the dragon and everything that he represents.

Dragons are mentioned by name, many times in the King James Bible. Some references to dragons include the following:

> I am a brother to dragons and companion to owls (Job 30:29).

> And the great dragon was cast out, that old serpent, called the Devil, and Satan, which deceiveth the whole world (Revelations 12:9).

The Bible lists several characteristics of dragons. This beast can be poisonous (Deuteronomy 32:33), and is quite powerful (Isaiah 27:1), and they are a symbol of evil and rebellion against God (Revelation 12:3-4).

Our life is full of dragons. We are faced with some type of dragon everyday. So you are asking, how so? With everyday challenges, obstacles and missed opportunities. With sickness, suffering, and loss of a job. Also, we have set-backs, financial strain, and evil attacks through lies and hatred. These are the attacks from the dragon.

But have no fear, Jesus Christ is the "Dragon-slayer". Isaiah 27 opens with the vision of the Lord slaying the sea monster Leviathan, the sea serpent Satan, the dragon, the devil. This creature was a monster of Egypt. The Lord is a "Dragon-slayer". The new exodus was then the slaying of the dragon Leviathan. It was when Jesus gave him a fatal blow to the head. Jesus did this to Satan with His death and resurrection.

Jesus defeats the enemies of God by satisfying the wrath of God. Jesus has already conquered the kingdom of Satan, and that resulted from Satan's accusations about us and our sins. Because of this, we have victory over our accuser. Jesus clothes us in His armor of His righteousness, by doing this, He shattered Satan's power of accusing us, now there is not condemnation for those who are in Jesus.

So whatever dragons you are facing in your life, give them to Jesus. Just trust Jesus and He will give you the strength, that you will need for your daily walk.

DISCONTENTMENT

Displeasure, dissatisfaction, disgruntlement, bitterness, resentment, uneasiness, the blues, dejection, depression, despondency, downheartedness, dreariness, the dumps, sadness, sorrow, plain outright summed all in one word, "DISCONTENTMENT."

DISCONTENTMENT! A sense of grievance. A restless desire or craving for something that you do not have. A longing for something to happen. "DISCONTENTMENT!" A lack of satisfaction with one's possessions, status, or situation.

We have all heard the saying over and over again, "that money can't buy you happiness." In our moments of discontent, we wish we can test that theory. The Bible clearly tells us, "Keep your life free from the love of money, and be content with what you have, for he has said, 'I will never leave you nor forsake you.'" (Hebrews 13:5)

We all struggle with being satisfied with our current situation. I am struggling now, as I wait on God to answer my prayer. So what is the cure for "Discontentment"? The answer is "gratitude," and having an attitude of gratitude. Thanking God for everything, the good and the bad. Apostle Paul says in Philippians 4:11, "Not that I speak in regard to need, for I have learned in whatever state I am, to be content."

When Paul penned those words above, he was in prison. So how could Apostle Paul be sitting in a dreadful place like prison, suffering and say, "in whatever situation I am, to be content? Paul was keeping his eyes on the prize and the Prize was Jesus Christ, which was the secret to Paul's contentment.

When we are in "discontentment", we grumble and complain. We start sulking, and with me on some occasions, I will go stomping around the house with my lips poked-out.

Just think about some of those gifts you received over the years. Some of them were crappy and some of them were great, but you still thanked the giver for the gift. Right?

God is our very good Giver for every gift that He gives us. We should thank Him for every occasion, in every situation.

When we are thankful, thankfulness changes our attitude and our outlook on life. We must always keep our spiritual eyes on the Prize, because when we look away, and look at what it looks like, what we start pondering on, is what we will perceive. We will become discontent because, we will start meditating on the wrong things, and these things will weigh us down, and will lead to frustration. Discontentment cannot coexist with humbled thankfulness.

We should always be thankful to God, day and night, for all things, the good and the bad, because God allowed it to happen. If He brought it to you, He will see you through it. Keep your eyes on the Prize, by fixing your eyes on Jesus. Jesus is the recipe for contentment.

FORGIVENESS

Have you ever been betrayed? I have, on many occasions. The more you care about the betrayer, the deeper the pain.

Have you noticed that the more you do for a person, the more they have the nerves to think that you are supposed to do it like you owe them something. When in fact you owe them absolutely nothing.

Sometimes people can be cruel and unkind. Sometimes people are unappreciative of your kindness. Sometimes people become angry with you for no reason. Sometimes people will mistreat you and can be unfair to you. So, what do you do? God says to forgive them and forget. Luke 6:37 says, "Judge not, and ye shall not be judged: condemn not, and ye shall not be condemned: forgive, and ye shall be forgiven."

Forgiveness is often defined as an individual, voluntary internal process of letting go of feelings and thoughts of resentment, bitterness, anger, and the need for vengeance and retribution toward someone who we believe has wronged us.

In forgiveness, Jesus tells us to be gracious to others because it is the right thing to do. He also tells us that perks come with doing so. So, what do you get when you forgive others? Benefits! You will be forgiven! What's in it for you if you avoid condemning others? You will get the rich benefits of not being condemned.

If we are critical rather than compassionate, we will also receive criticism. If you treat others generously and graciously, it is a boomerang effect, it is coming back to you. We are to love others and forgive them and not judge.

Forgiveness is a choice you make and you have to make that choice over and over again.

Forgiveness is a gift to others and to yourself. A forgiving heart places you on a different stratosphere and marks you as a cut above the rest. In other words, having a forgiving heart makes you a "Super Hero". Forgiveness gives you wings to help you move forward.

Forgiveness puts you in an entirely different group. You become part of a "Masterclass". Mastering the art of love, the love of Christ, and to love others.

THE ALL PURPOSE CLEANER

An all purpose cleaner is a multi-purpose liquid, spray-on cleaner that can be used on several types of dirt. It is one of the most common products used by a detailer.

It sounds like a wonderful and awesome product: the all purpose cleaner (or multi-purpose cleaner) that typically does away with many of the hassles associated with cleaning. There is no need to store five separate bottles of expensive cleaning products, when just the one will do. No more reading instruction labels to see what cleans what, just take the all purpose cleaner and spray. And wala!

What does an all purpose cleaner do? In short, an all purpose cleaner is designed to be used on many different surfaces and for a variety of cleaning tasks around the house. There is actually, no standard set of ingredients for those types of cleaners, but they act as either a disinfectant, detergent, degreaser, or solvent or a combination of all of those.

Doesn't this sounds absolutely amazing? There is only ONE that can clean anything and everything. His cleaning abilities is better, far more excellent than any man-made product. I am talking about the amazing "Wonder Cleaner," the original "All Purpose Cleaner", and His name is JESUS!

J-E-S-U-S: Jesus-Erases-Sins-Ugly Sins.
J-E-S-U-S: Jesus-Erases-Sins-Undisclosed-Sins.
J-E-S-U-S: Jesus-Erases-Sins0Unacceptable-Sins.
J-E-S-U-S: Jesus-Erases-Sins-Unimaginable-Sins.
J-E-S-U-S: Jesus-Erases-Sins-Unquestionable-Sins.

God promised a day when He would completely purify us. "Then it will be as though I had sprinkled clean water on you, for you will be clean-your filthiness will be washed away, your idol worship gone. And I will give you a new heart - I will give you new and right desires — and put a new spirit within you. I will take out your stony hearts of sin and give you new hearts of love. And I will put my Spirit within you so that you will obey my laws and do whatever I command" Ezekiel 36:25-27.

Sin has soiled us and God promises to wash us. He promised that our bodies will be cleanse, our minds will be cleansed, and our hearts will be cleansed. Cleansed from what?

Our bodies bears the filth of sin. Our bodies are the temple of the lIving God. It carries a stain and a stench that soap can't remove. Only Jesus can erase the guilt and shame that pollutes our bodies.

Our minds becomes filled with evil thoughts. Wrong attitudes contaminate our minds. We become trapped by images from what we read and what we watch in the movies and on television. God can change our thought process.

Our unclean heart! Sin is originated in our hearts. The natural inclination from the natural man/ woman, lives inside us. Only Jesus, himself can purify us. "…Cleanse me

with hyssop, and I will be clean, wash me, and I will be whiter than snow" (Psalm 51:7).

The Holy Spirit can and will wash away the stench from our body, mind, heart and soul. God is the original " All Purpose Cleaner".

GOSSIP

Do you gossip? Have you ever participated in gossip? Have you ever been the recipient of gossip?

Romans 1:29 says, "being filled with all unrighteousness, wickedness, greed, evil, full of envy, murder, strife, deceit, malice, they are gossip".

Gossip is an exaggeration, or a fabrication of a story, or a lie, regarding someone other than the person who is telling it. The person who is telling it, is called a "talebearer" and they are discussing someone, normally, for a malicious purpose, to demean, slander, or tarnish their reputation.

Gossipers are those people who like to talk about other people's private or personal business. They are busybodies, gossipmongers, meddlers, and rumormongers. They like to throw dirt on people. They spread hear-says. They divide and conquer with rumors and scandal. Their chit-chat, are full of idle conversations while telling tales, dishing the dirt, talking out of turn, while they spill the tea.

Many people profits from the spread of gossip. There are "gossip columnists" and "gossip blogs".

Everyone has experienced the hurt from gossip. Some people meant to cause harm, and some didn't. The result of gossip causes broken trust, hurt feelings, and ruined reputations.

Let me share a story about "The Triple Filter Test". Socrates was visited by an acquaintance of his. Eager to share some juicy gossip, the man asked if Socrates would like to know the story he'd just heard about a friend of theirs. Socrates replied that before the man spoke, he needed to pass "The Triple-Filter Test".

The first filter, he explained, is Truth. "Have you made absolutely sure that what you are about to say is true? The man shook his head. "No, I actually just heard about it, and ..."

Socrates cut him off. "You don't know for certain that it is true, then, is what you want to say, is it good or kind? Again, the man shook his head. "No! Actually, just the opposite. You see..."

Socrates lifted his hand to stop the man from speaking. "So you are not certain that what you want to say is true, and it isn't good or kind." One filter still remains, though, so you may yet still tell me. Is this information, useful or necessary to me? A little defeated, the man replied, "No, not really."

"Well, then, "Socrates said, turning on his heels. If what you want to say is neither true, nor good or kind, nor useful or necessary, please don't say anything at all."

Words are powerful. Words can build someone up or tear them down. When you spread a malicious rumor, you commit character assassination. Something like this can have a tremendous negative effect on someone.

God's word warns us to stay away from people who gossip. God tells us to guard our words when we speak about others.

So, lets' take a movement. If it doesn't fit "The Triple Filter Test," don't listen and don't spread it. But if you need to gossip, let's gossip about the "good news" of Jesus Christ.

God's scripture warns us about making false statements that can damage a person's reputation. That word in the Bible is called, SLANDER. Slander can destroy a person's life, marriage, family, and career. The tongue is a powerful weapon. The Bible warns us of what words to speak and what not to speak.

THE TWO ME'S

There is a battle going on within. The battle within, is a fierce battle and we are faced with this battle often. We can make ourselves stronger within, or we can destroy ourselves from within. "The toughest battle you'll ever fight in your life is the battle within yourself."

Jesse Owens stated, "The battles that count aren't the ones for gold medals. The struggles within yourself, the invisible, inevitable battles inside all of us, that's where it's at."

Apostle Paul wrote, "I do not understand what I do. For what I want to do I do not do, but what I hate to do. And if I do what I do not want to do, I agree that the law is good. As it is, it is no longer I myself who do it, but it is sin living in me. I know that good itself does not dwell in me, that is, in my sinful nature. For I have the desire to do what is good, but I cannot carry it out. For I do not do the good I want to do but the evil I do not want to do — this I keep on doing" (Romans 7:15-19).

I am so very hard on myself. There is always a battle going on within me. There is the "Can Do Me" and there is the "I Can't Do It Me." I call the "Can Do Me," the Big Me, and the "I Can't Do It," the little Me. The Little Me is negative and doubtful, and the Big Me is positive and full of confidence. I have to fight very hard for the Big Me.

For us Christians, we need to allow the Big Me to take over when doubt and uncertainty creeps in.

Scripture makes it clear that there is a warfare going on inside of every Believer. Why? Because there are two natures inside us battling to sit on the throne of our lives. The first nature is the one that comes with natural birth.

When we are self-centered, self-absorbed, self-focused, and we desire to be self-ruled. But when by grace, through faith, we are raised from the dead to life, we are given a new nature that begins to do battle with the old. It is through our regeneration that the battle begins, setting up the fight of the new nature, with the old nature.

That's why the Bible tells us to "live by the Spirit" and we will not gratify the desires of the sinful nature. For the sinful nature desires what is contrary to the Spirit, and the Spirit what is contrary to the sinful nature. They are in conflict with each other. We must remember that our new nature is absolutely perfect in Christ. It is spotless, blameless, and righteous. It is incapable of sinning because it is the nature of God.

It's easy to figure out which of our two natures will gain the upper hand, in the war within. It is the one we feed. If we are more focused on the things of this world, our sinful nature will get the upper hand. But if you keep your eyes fixed on the things that are above, our new nature will win the prize.

So, there you have it! Let's starve the Little Me and feed the Big Me. When we focus on things above, we will rise above the battle within and allow God to feed our souls. With God, we are always on the winning team. WINNING!

TREASURE HUNT

Do you know what a treasure hunt is? A treasure hunt means to search for treasures. A treasure hunt is a game in which each person attempts to be first in finding something that has been hidden.

As children, we use to play this game. The goal of the game was to lead us through a set of clues that would take us from place to place to find a treasure. We would read each clue that we found, and try to figure out the next location.

Example:

Clue #1- Keeping food cold is important you see. This is the place where the milk will be.

Clue #2 - "Ding Dong" is the sound that comes from this place. It means that someone is here to see you, face to face.

Do you know that there is a Godly treasure hunt? Absolutely so! King Solomon, the wisest man who ever lived, left us a legacy of written wisdom in three volumes; Proverbs, Ecclesiastes, and the Song of Solomon. In these three books, under the inspiration of the Holy Spirit, he gives practical insights and guidelines for life.

Yes, if you want better insight and discernment, and if you search for them as would for lost money or hidden treasure, then wisdom will be given to you, and knowledge of God himself. "For the Lord grants wisdom! His every word is a treasure of knowledge and understanding."

Wisdom is both a God-given gift and an energetic search. Wisdom's starting point, is God and his Word, the "treasure of knowledge and understanding". In this sense, it is his gift to us. But he gives it only to those who earnestly seek it. The pathway to wisdom is strenuous. When we are searching for it, we discover that true wisdom belongs to God, and that we cannot create it by our own efforts.

Wisdom comes through a constant process of growth. First, we must trust and honor God. Second, we must realize that the Bible reveals God's wisdom to us. Third, we must make a lifelong series of right choices. Fourth, when we make a mistake, and we will, we must learn from it.

Knowledge is good, but there is a vast difference between knowledge (having the facts), and wisdom (applying those facts to your life). We may amass knowledge, but without wisdom, our knowledge is useless.

The person who has Wisdom is loyal, kind, trusts in the Lord, puts God first, turn from evil, knows right from wrong, listens, and learns, and does what is right.

When we choose God's way, he grants us wisdom. "Wisdom gives: A long, good life, riches, honor, pleasure, peace." (Proverbs 3:17)

Wisdom! What a treasure to search for. It is worth the treasure hunt.

ONE AND DONE

We only have one life to live on this earth. It is a "one and done" life.

Once it's "one and done," it is accomplished, completed, concluded, consummated, ended, executed, finished, over, perfected, realized, ready, finished, and through.

You only have one life to live, on this earth. "For what is your life? It is even a vapor that appears for a little time and then vanishes away" James 4:14 NKJV.

Life is too precious to waste. Life is a gift that has been given to each of us and we should make the most of it, with Christ. God gave us this wonderful gift of life and He also tells us, how we should live our life. He wants us to be careful of how we talk and walk. We are supposed to live a life, purposefully and worthily, and not unwise and foolishly.

Live purposely, is to live a life guided by His purpose. A purpose is something that you live for, a reason for the things that you do.

The Bible says that our purpose of life, is to love and trust and obey, God. To trust that He has nothing but love for us, and He would not tell us to do something, without a good reason, and for our good. In Ecclesiastes 12:13, King Solomon wrote, 'The conclusion of the matter, everything have been heard, is: Fear the true God and keep his commandments, for this is the whole obligation of man." Serving God and keeping his commands is not only the whole obligation of mankind, but it also our purpose.

We were created for God's glory and honor. God created us in His image and likeness. Now since He created us to look like him, He would want us to act like him, to love like Him, to treat people the way he would treat them. He want us to love Him first, then love one another, as He loves us.

Our purpose is to glorify God and enjoy Him forever. How do we glorify God? We glorify God by fearing and obeying Him. By keeping our eyes on our future home, that is in heaven. We are supposed to develop a relationship with God, not just any kind of relationship, but an intimate relationship.

God wants us to stay in-tuned with him, by talking to him and making him inclusive in our lives. He wants to be included and part of every single detail. The small, trivial things and the most important ones as well. He loves us and enjoys us and He wants us to follow His purpose for our lives. This enables us to experience true and lasting joy, the kind of joy that only He can give. He desires that we have an abundant life because He wants the best for us. And when our life is over, we will see him in our next life, in our heavenly home, and there we can behold God's face and fellowship with Him, in our new heavenly bodies.

WHAT DOES GOD REQUIRE OF YOU

What do you think that God expects from you? What is God's expectations of us? "He hath showed thee, O man, what is good: and what doth the Lord require of thee, but to do justly, and to love mercy, and to walk humbly with thy God?" Micah 6:8.

God has a "Rulebook" for us. A "Rulebook" is a collection of rules or prescribed standards on the basis of which decisions are made and may I add, the way we should live our lives.

We know what God does and doesn't want us to do. Do not lie. Do not steal. Do not commit adultery. Do not murder. Do not covet what others have. Do not dishonor your mother and father. Do not use His name in vain. Do not worship any other god, but Him. These are the "DO NOTs".

There are some "DOs". He does expect us to love Him with all of our heart, soul, strength and mind. He does want us to love others as we love ourselves, and love others as Jesus loves us.

Those are the do's and don'ts. God has given us the "rulebook" for living on this earth. The "rulebook" is His Holy Bible.

But what is God's ultimate expectations from us? God expects us to accept His Son, the Lord Jesus Christ, as our Savior. He expects us to give our lives to Him and in doing this, we will develop His character.

What character? Jesus combines majesty with the greatest humility. He put together the strongest commitment to justice and mercy. Then He reveals to us self-sufficiency and yet an entirely trust in our Heavenly Father. The Bible shows us His tenderness without any weakness. We see His boldness without any harshness. He insists on showing us the TRUTH, showered in His LOVE. He shows us His power, with sensitivity and integrity. He shows us passion, without any prejudice. There was no respect of man. He welcomed and ate with prostitutes. He touched the lepers, those that was considered physically and ceremonially uncleaned. He showed that he was not a bigot toward the bigoted, those Pharisees when he ate with them.

He welcomed and befriended all, while surprisingly witnessing the truth, even to Zacchaeus, the despised tax collector. When He encountered women who were sexually immoral, he engaged with them with respect, but He gently pointed out to the Samaritan woman the error of her ways.

Jesus is full of grace, mercy, compassion, and He is the TRUTH. God wants us to develop the character of His beloved Son, Jesus. Jesus' character traits were humble service, holiness, righteousness, purity, love, forgiveness, compassion, endurance, submission, humility, obedient, kindness, generous giving, meek, and prayerful, just to name a few.

In order to be like Jesus we must conformed or transformed into His image. We must emulate Him. God expects for us to put on the character of Jesus. How do you do this? By building your life on the teachings of Jesus, by applying the principles of Scriptures to our thoughts and conduct, conforming through transforming to the will of God, and not of the world.

When we allow God to mold us and renew our mind, a transformation will occur and we will take on the qualities of God's character.

A GOOD WORD

Appreciation, gratitude, inspiring, possibilities, succeed, values, respectful, joy, compassion, believe, creative, love, joyfulness, peace, motivate, goodness, happy, fearless, hope, and empower are some examples of some "good words".

Proverbs 15:4, "Gentle words bring life and health; a deceitful tongue crushes the spirit."

Without words a thought would be difficult to become a reality. Words have energy and power and the ability to help, heal, hurt, humiliate, and humble.

Words have power. Words can be positive and beautiful. Words can lift someone up and words can tear someone down. Words have the ability to change lives. Words can build up a relationship and words can destroy a relationship. Words can bring peace and words can create wars.

Words can create a reality too. Did you know that we will be accountable before God, for every word that comes out of our mouth? Matthew 12:36 says, "And I tell you this, that you must give account on Judgment Day for every word you speak. Your words now reflect your fate then: either you will be justified by them or you will be condemned."

Jesus reminds us that what we say reveals what is in our hearts. So what kind of words come from your mouth? That is an indication of what your heart is really like. The mouth says what the heart feels. You can clean your speech up, but if the heart hasn't changed, there is still a problem with the heart. Only the Holy Spirit can change your heart. He can put a transforming power on your heart, which is better than a heart transplant. "A good word makes the heart glad." (Proverbs 12:25)

Where can you get a "good word?" Philippians 4:8 tells us, "Fix your thoughts on what is true and good and right. Think about things that are pure and lovely, and dwell on the fine, good things in others." This is a "good word."

What we put into our minds also, determines what comes out in our words and through our actions. Examine what you are putting into your mind through books, movies, and television. Above all, read God's Word, the Bible. Pray daily, sing songs — praising songs, and practice saying encouraging words.

These "good words" will bring joy and peace to your heart through the Holy Spirit.

JOY AND PAIN

Joy and pain. Sunshine and rain. Joy and pain, what a combination. When in times of joy, everything seems so bright. Sometimes amid the hustle and bustle of life, we temporarily forfeit the joy of Christ as we wrestle with our daily living.

Every human alive has dealt with these two emotions, joy, and pain. What is joy? Joy is a feeling of great pleasure and happiness, according to the Oxford dictionary. Galatians 5:22-23 gives us a list of the fruits of the spirit and joy is listed there as one of the products of the Holy Spirit, living and abiding within us.

God alone can produce true joy and it is God who can give us the ability to respond to life's difficulties. We will all have to face sorrow, pain, and grief. We will all have trials and troubles. Trials will beset our every step. We are bowed down with trouble, sadness, pain, and sorrow and our eyes become wet with tears.

I praise our Heavenly Father, that He comforts us through every trial, trouble, sorrow, and pain. God through His great mercy is always there to help us get through anything and everything.

Some of us are sick and in distress. Some of us have thoughts that are full of negativity and bitterness and anxiety. God can console you. He can provide you with comfort, peace, and joy. Only God can turn those frowns upside down, into smiles.

2 Corinthians 1:3 says, "Praise be to the God and Father of our Lord Jesus Christ, the Father of compassion and the God of all comfort, who comforts us in all our troubles so that we can comfort those in any trouble with the comfort we ourselves receive from God."

Joy and pain, two sentiments that are totally opposite from each other, and yet, it appears that they go hand in hand. One moment you are in total bliss filled with joy and the next moment, you feel nothing but pain. We all have experienced some pain in our lives, whether emotionally or physically. No, two people, pain is alike, but as sure as we are alive, we all will have to walk this path.

God tells us that there is a purpose for our pain. We can't understand its purpose while we are going through the pain, but mama would say, "hindsight is 20/20."

With God's help, we can press on knowing that God loves us and is always with us. God wants to use our hurt and pain to bring Him glory. The Bible is full of scriptures to help us understand the purpose of our pain and will encourage us on how to find joy in the midst of our suffering.

Joy and pain. We rejoice sometimes and we weep sometimes. At times it may appear that we are doing both simultaneously because life is bitter and sweet, full of joy and yet there is so much pain.

As a child of God, He has equipped us for the joyful days and the painful days. In our weakness and pain, we are carried by the joy in the Lord. He is our strength and our salvation.

Jesus is our Redeemer and our pain and our joy are meaningful because of Him. You can press your pain into His joy and let it ignite your joy into a joyful fire and this will save you from the depths of your pain.

I DO NOT UNDERSTAND

As a child, when my mother said, "NO" to me, I did not understand why so many simple requests from me came with an answer of "NO".

I remembered mulling over the answer "NO" from my mother. I just did not get it. It made no sense to me. It was completely beyond me, and for a long time, I just couldn't understand why I couldn't have my way from some simple request.

Abraham could not understand why God would ask him to sacrifice his son, but he trusted God. Moses could not understand why God kept him in the wilderness for forty years, but he trusted God. Joseph could not understand why his brothers would sell him into slavery, and why Potiphar's wife would lie on him with imprisonment for punishment, but he trusted God. Mary and Martha could not understand why Jesus would let their beloved brother die, but Jesus told them, "You may not understand; but I tell you if you believe, you will see."

Sometimes, some things happen and we just don't understand. Sometimes, it may seem like life just doesn't make sense. Why does God allow bad things to happen? Why some people live to 100, while others die young? Why do natural disasters happen? Why is it taking God so long to answer our prayers?

As we cry out to God and ask questions, because we do not understand, and we are feeling some kind of a way, and yet, we know that we serve a loving and living God, whose love for us is completely incomprehensible. We are still hopeful and we are comforted, knowing that although we do not understand, God does.

Isaiah 55:8-9 says, "For my thoughts are not your thoughts, neither are your ways my ways, declared the Lord. For as the heavens are higher than the earth, so are my ways higher than your ways and my thoughts than your thoughts."

God knows and God understands. It may not make sense to us, but it makes perfectly good sense to God. There are somethings that we just don't have the capacity to fully understand. God may have allowed something to happen, but it doesn't mean it makes God happy. Life doesn't make sense at times, but we can go to the ONE who knows all and sees all. When we don't understand, but we can trust the ONE who understands.

We may feel heart broken. We may even think that God has forgotten us. Please don't feel that way, because God will never forget about you. God loves you and He cares very much about you. Please do not give up! Please do not stop trusting God! Please do not turn away from God! This is the time to run to Him.

We will never understand God's ways, and God doesn't expect us to understand them. Just like, when I was a child, I didn't understand why my mother would always say "NO", to me. Just like my son did not understand why I would say "NO", sometimes to him, on so many occasions. I was only protecting him from himself and that was what my mother was doing for me. As a child of God, we may not understand, we just need to believe that He is working for our good. In due season, we will see the glory of God, in the things that we did not understand.

THE THREE D'S

So you woke up this morning and is faced with another day with Despair, Doubt, and Disappointment. You stopped to ask yourself how did these three get here? You thought that you had left them behind you last night. You thought that you had placed them in your emotional trunk and locked them away. But who greeted you this morning all droopy eyes telling dreary tales? Why of course, it was Despair, Doubt, and Disappointment. They were live and in action. They redefined what a tag-team is all about. You continue questioning yourself, how did I get here? I never should have been here. What am I doing here?

You are not alone. Many people are feeling the same way you are feeling and is questioning themselves too. In 1 Kings 19, Elijah found God asking him, "Elijah what are you doing here?"

Elijah found himself in a situation that had him in despair, doubt, and disappointment. Really? Oh yes! He was hiding in the wilderness. Are there times in your life that you wish that you can hide until everything that is going wrong can be worked out? Maybe you haven't felt this way, but I have.

Queen Jezebel was an enemy of Elijah and she was out to harm him. Despair, doubt, and disappointment were overwhelming him, but God had a plan for Elijah. Elijah knew the power of God because he had devoted his life in proving God's power. But there Elijah was, alone in the wilderness, hiding out and prayed that he might die. Elijah said, "I have had enough," he told the Lord. "Take away my life, I have got to die sometime, and it might as well be now" (verse 4).

Then God asked the question, "What are you doing here, Elijah?" God proceeded to show Elijah his powers, through the windstorm, through the earthquake, and through the fire. But God wasn't in those, He was in the sound of a gentle whisper, a "still small voice." Then God asked him again, "What are you doing here, Elijah?"

Elijah poured his heart out, "I have been working very hard for the Lord God of the armies of heaven, but the people have broken their covenant and have torn down your altars; they have killed every one of your prophets except me: and now they are trying to kill me too" (verse 14). In other words, he was wandering, how did God let him get into this situation? After all he was a very dedicated soldier for God.

Have you ever given your "all in all," only to have things turned out unexpectedly? Have you spent your life being a dedicated soldier for Christ and every time you look around you find yourself in turbulence. Maybe there was a misunderstanding or an innocent situation got out of control and people blamed you and blew it out of proportion. Those type of things will cause despair, doubt, and disappointment.

When doubt, despair, and disappointment confronts you and persist to tag along, take them to Jesus, and He will lift you up and place you in His peace, contentment, and wonder. He will transform despair, doubt, and disappointment into desire, dedication, and determination.

HOPE, HOPING, HOPEFUL

WHAT IS HOPE?

Hope is an optimistic state of mind that is based on an expectation of positive outcomes with respect to events, and circumstances in one's life or the world at large. As a verb, its definition includes: "expect with confidence" and "to cherish a desire with anticipation."

WHAT IS HOPE, EXACTLY?

When people talk about hope in a spiritual context it means, believing good things will happen with faith in God. The Bible says, "Now may God of hope fill you with all joy and peace in believing, so that you will abound in hope by the power of the Holy Spirit" Romans 15:13.

"HOPE" is commonly used to mean a wish: its strength of the person's desire. But in the Bible "hope" is the confident expectation of what God has promised and its strength is in His faithfulness.

WHY IS HOPE IMPORTANT?

We need "HOPE" to motivate us. Hope is the unshakeable belief that no matter how bad our circumstance, that somehow, someway, everything will turn out all right.

There are somethings that we can live with and there are somethings that we cannot live without. We can live a few minutes without air. We can live a few days without water. We can live a few days, maybe a few weeks without food. Some of us can live at length without being loved and being in love. But I don't think that we can live without "HOPE."

Everybody hope for something. When people are having problems in life, they "hope." If you are looking for a job, you "hope." When dating, you "hope" that it will go further. When you apply for a loan, you "hope." When you take a test, you "hope."

HOPE, is given by a doctor to their patients.
HOPE, is a necessity for the poor and needy.
HOPE, is like an energizer for those who are fighting depression.
HOPE, is needed as a life-line in a troubled marriage.
HOPE, is needed for parents raising their children.
HOPE, is needed for a lost soul that they will give their life to Christ.
HOPE, is needed for people who are facing difficulties in their lives.

HOPE, is absolutely needed for a vaccine for COVID-19.

Now, I know that what I hope for, I can be confident it will come to pass. I can hope and believe that God will keep me in perfect peace for those whose minds are steadfast, because I trust him. I can hope and have faith that God will instruct me and teach me in the ways I should go. I hope and believe that the Lord will fight for me, if I only be still. I hope and know, that in all things God works for the good of those who love him, who have been called according to His purpose. I hope and know that Jesus gives strength to the weary and increases the power of the weak. I hope and believe that no weapon forged against me will prevail, and I will refute every tongue that accuses me.

HOPE is real! Hope is limitless! Hope is alive! Let's keep HOPE alive! GOD is hope! God truly is the God of HOPE!

To cut someone out means to separate them from things that they are normally connected with.

To cut out is to sever, separate, disinherit, amputate, chop-off, disendow, tear-out, and to remove.

There are some people in your life that aren't good for you. You are not equally yoked. They are trouble makers, nay-sayers, negative, abusive, and emotionally detached. They are full of criticism, insults, and they are just outright TOXIC.

Psychological research shows that criticism and insults are five times more powerful than compliments. That means if you want to keep any type of friendship, relationship, or marriage flourishing with them, you will need five positive reactions or interactions, for every negative one.

So what do you do to minimize your interaction with these types of people? Simply, if they are in your life, just CUT THEM OUT. I personally will not associate with the negative kind. I try to avoid these types of people because those people's energy is toxic and I will try to avoid them, like the plague.

My circle is very small, it's not an accident, it is by design. I have made a conscious decision a long time ago, to be careful about who I surround myself with. We need to choose our friends very carefully. So, who have you surrounded yourself with?

"He who walks with wise men will be wise, but the companion of fools will be destroyed" (Proverbs 13:20).

If you surround yourself with wise people, you will allow yourself to be influenced by those who are wise. If you are a companion of fools, even if you are not aware of it, you will be influenced by them. You don't have to do anything wrong, it's a proximity thing. There is an old proverb that says, "Birds of a feather flock together." This means, people of similar character, background, or taste tend to congregate or associate with one another.

I pride myself on being a woman of God. I believe in giving every-one the" benefit of the doubt." So when your true self is revealed, and I realized that nothing that I can say to encourage you to see it Jesus' way, then I have to "CUT THEM OUT," and keep it moving.

Our daily prayer should be, 'Lord is there is anything in me that should not be, please "CUT IT OUT!"

ENVY - CUT IT OUT!

JEALOUSY - CUT IT OUT!

PRIDE - CUT IT OUT!

BACKBITING - CUT IT OUT!

EXCUSES - CUT IT OUT!

ARROGANCE - CUT IT OUT!

DISOBEDIENCE - CUT IT OUT!

LYING - CUT IT OUT!

LUSTING - CUT IT OUT!

Child of God, be on the look-out for the following:

1) Gossipers: these types will deliberately tear people down, including you.
2) Emotional Vampires: they comes in different forms. Some will elicit pity for problems they really don't want to solve. Some just like to make you miserable.
3) The Green-eye Monster: Jealousy is a very evil spirit. These people will pretend like they are happy for you, but they are not.

If it doesn't glorify God, simply "CUT IT OUT!"

THE LOVE OF MONEY

Money is a medium of exchange. It allows people to obtain what they need to live. Like gold and other precious metals, money has its worth because for most people it represents something valuable.

Money makes the world go around. Economies rely on the exchange of money for products and services. The value of money is decided by its purchasing power. Money is valuable because we want it, but we want it because it can get us what we want.

You have heard the phrase, "for the love of money is the root of evil." This phrase is misquoted. "For the love of money is a root of all sorts of evil, and some by longing for it has wandered away from the faith and pierced themselves with many griefs" 1 Timothy 6:10.

The Bible did not say that money is the root of all evil, but "the love of money" is. Money is mentioned over 800 times in the Bible. Money and possessions are the second most referenced topic in the Bible.

Most people still believe that money brings about happiness. Our society is in love with money and the things that money can buy. Rich people crave greater riches. Poor people will almost kill for it. Some people have sold their souls for it. Some people worship money. They are all about the "benjamins," "the mean green," the "almighty dollar."

There is nothing almighty about the dollar. Only God is "almighty," not the dollar. You can't have a love for money and love Jesus. That cannot exist. We are to love God with all of our hearts, with all our souls, with all our minds, and with all our strength. We are to love our neighbors as ourselves.

When you love money, your desires are on the money. It means that your emotions are attached to money. The affection of your heart is centered on money, its power, its security, and you are trusting in it.

You can't love Jesus and money also. Money in and of itself is not evil, but worshipping it is. When we worship God, we are truly blessed. Loving Jesus means that you wake up every day with a commitment to live your life to satisfy Him. Your emotions are centered on Him. You know that you can trust Him to comfort you, lead you, guide you, sustain you, and to provide for you. You know that God will fill you with His power, and give you His peace.

No, there is nothing "mighty" about the dollar, but we worship and praise a "Mighty God" who is "ALMIGHTY".

ave you ever witnessed a storm? Have you ever found yourself in the middle of a storm?

On October 29, 2020, Tropical Storm ZETA made US land on Wednesday afternoon as a category 2 hurricane, lashing the Louisiana coast. Heavy rain and damaging winds from Zeta swept through North Georgia, including Atlanta on Thursday morning, leaving a least three people dead and nearly 1 million people in the dark.

All across the metro area, fallen trees and downed wires, temporality blocked interstates, disabled traffic signals and shut down the local streets.

In life we go through many storms. Where there is no literal lightening or thunder, rain or wind, but it truly feels that way. Figurative, lightening passes and frightens us through fears of uncertainty. The wind blows discomfort and distress upon us. Thunder with its thunderstorms showers us with disappointments and discord. We become caught up in a spiritual and emotional storm.

I wish I can tell you that by following Jesus, that you will never be troubled again, but I can't. Life and being a Christian appears to come with trouble. Life is full of ups and downs, with some twists and turns, and there will be love and loss.

Life doesn't play out as we plan. One moment everything is silky smooth, then the next moment, your life is full of chaos. There will be times that your bad days will have bad days.

Jesus said there will be days, weeks, months, maybe years like this. Psalm 23:4 says, "Yea, though I walk through the valley of the shadow of death, I will fear no evil; for You are with me; Your rod and Your staff, they comfort me." Verse 4 reminds us that when we are walking through the storm (hard times), God is always near and is there to protect and comfort us.

As you face the storms in your life, Jesus is always there with you and for you. You are never alone. Whatever the situation, God is there to comfort and guide you. So don't look at the problems, just focus on God's promises. When you focus only on the problems, you will lose sight of God's promises.

"Peace Be Still!" One of the best known stories in the Gospels (Matthew 8:23-27) is that of Jesus calming the storm on the lake. There we see that Jesus demonstrated His authority over the elements of nature.

This same Jesus, who is Lord of lords and King of kings, in the days of old, is the same Jesus today. He is still controlling everything in heaven, earth, and under the earth.

Jesus didn't promise us that our lives would be smooth sailing, but He did promise us that He would be our shelter in the midst of a storm.

So, if your life is in a storm, please remember that Jesus will get you to the other side. You have His word on it. For He said, "I will never leave you nor forsake you" (Hebrews 13:5).

Jesus is "THE SHELTER" in the midst of a storm.

DIS-EASE

When God wants you to grow, He will make you feel uncomfortable. I am feeling uncomfortable now because I know that I am going through a metamorphosis. Metamorphosis is a change of the form or nature of a thing or person into a completely different one by natural or supernatural means.

Dis-ease is the biggest killer of progress. If you want a chance of living an extraordinary life, you will have to experience some dis-ease and this will make you feel very uncomfortable.

We will go to any length to avoid pain and feeling uncomfortable. We do want pleasure, but unfortunately, this may cause you to just settle for mediocrity. Settling will lead to a whole host of problems and will prevent you from living in your purpose. I mean literally walking into your purpose.

I hate to tell you, but growth comes with a price. Believe it or not, there is opportunity in adversity. While God is preparing you to walking into your purpose, at the right moment, this will bring about a difficult time in your life. This time is a very interesting time and is a crucial part of getting the best out of your life. At that moment, goals, accomplishments, and victory will also become obtainable.

When you become uncomfortable, that is when you start growing. God will give you opportunities, but it is up to you if you accept them. It is up to you, as to what you will do with them. You will find yourself in a "use it" or "lose it" situation. God will not force you into it. He will just open the door for you to walk through, to go and get it. When the door is opened, only you can go and get it.

The only way to obtain your dream, you will have to go through a little discomfort. Your purpose, your dream, is just one step away from your comfort zone. Just one step away! When you make that one step, the magic begins to happen: that frightening job interview may give you a shot at your dream job; the initiative to start your business or product line is just one step away; or publishing your books may give you a chance to make a difference in someone's life.

"Growth is often uncomfortable, messy, and full of feelings you were not expecting, but it is necessary."

"For I know the plans I have for you, declares the Lord, plans for welfare and not for evil, to give you a future and a hope" (Jeremiah 29:11).

God has a habit of calling those He loves into difficult situations. He called Abraham to leave his home and to wander around in a strange land. He called Moses to stand before Pharaoh. He allowed Daniel to be tossed in the lion's den, because he kept praying despite a decree.

So why do you think that you can get "off the hook?" No one wants to be uncomfortable, especially me. Many of us experience "dis-ease" in our daily life. Being a Christian isn't easy and the life of faith and obedience is not a comfortable one. As a child of God, our life will be rich, because it is saturated with the power, presence, and provisions of God.

What is God calling you to do today? Is He offering you comfort or dis-ease? Remember, there is opportunity in adversity and dis-ease.

CPR! Yes, CPR! There are different acronyms for CPR. First, there is CPR, Cell Phone Repair. CPR - Cell Phone Repair was founded in 2004 and began franchising in 2007. CPR franchise locations offer walk-in, drop-off, and mail-in repair services for cell phones and other electronic devices.

CPR? The second type of CPR is cardiopulmonary resuscitation. This is an emergency life-saving procedure performed when the heart stops beating. Immediate CPR can double or triple the chances of survival of cardiac arrest. It combines chest compression, often with artificial ventilation, in an effort to manually preserve intact brain function, until further measures are taken to restore spontaneous blood circulation, and breathing in a person who is in cardiac arrest.

CPR, some people know CPR techniques and some people don't. CPR is like life insurance, it doesn't benefit you, because you can't use it on yourself, it benefits someone else. Some people really are in need of CPR, not the physical technique, but a Spiritual CPR. Someone needs a Spiritual Resuscitation. The church is in dire need of a Spiritual CPR. Some people need God to breathe on them, because they need to be revived, particularly, a revival of the soul. It's not that they are spiritually dead, but maybe they need some emergency attention from God.

Some people have been down for so long, they don't think that they can get back up. They need to be recharged and/or resuscitated So, how can that happen? God is a heart fixer and a mind regulator. Simply ask God for help, and He will help you.

Matthew 7:7 says, "Ask, and it will be given to you; seek, and you will find; knock, and it will be opened to you." In other words, Matthew 7:7 says, just ask, then keep asking; then seek and keep on seeking; then knock and keep knocking. God will answer your prayers. CPR means to Continue, to Pray, then Rejoice.

There is perseverance and diligence in prayer, as you learn endurance and discipline in waiting. I know some of us have had so many challenges and we are still waiting on God to answer our prayers. Some of us have been praying and waiting so long, we feel like our prayer life needs to be placed on a "life support machine." For some of you, your faith has wavered and you feel like your trust in Christ may need a "defibrillator". You must Persist and Persevere in Prayer.

Prayer breathes life back into a dead situation and circumstance. It shocks your heart into life, so it can operate as it should. It confronts you with the reason why Jesus died on the cross for you. The cross of Jesus allows God to have His finger on your pulse and allow your heart to beat as it should. The resurrected power, offers resuscitation power. What a jumpstart to the heart! God's CPR offers you, Compassion, Promises, and Restoration POWER. God will never break a promise, because John 15:7 says, "But if you remain in me and my words remain in you, you may ask for anything you want, and it will be granted!"

So as children of God what does CPR really mean to us in times of crisis? CPR means, there will be "Challenges", you should always "Pray", and after prayer, you should "Rejoice".

Moses was not only a great prophet but a song-leader as well. After three sermons, he changed the form of his message in Deuteronomy, chapter 32, to singing.

Moses wrote the words, but God is the author of these words, "Vengeance is mine, and I will repay. In due time their foot will slip; their day of disaster is near and their doom rushes upon them" (Deuteronomy 32:35).

Now in case you are saying that this is an Old Testament scripture and it doesn't reflect the gospel of today, wait just a minute, let me share this with you. It is repeated again in the New Testament in Romans 12:19-21, "Beloved, do not avenge yourselves, but rather give place to wrath; for it is written, 'Vengeance is Mine, I will re-pay,' says the Lord. Therefore "If your enemy hungers, feed him; if he thirsts, give him a drink; for in so doing you will heap coals of fire on his head." Do not be overcome by evil, but overcome evil with good."

In verse 19, the phrase, "…do not avenge yourselves, but rather give place to wrath…Vengeance is mine…" Paul is saying, "Leave it to the wrath of God." Then God goes to say, "I will repay." God's wrath is repayment to whoever wrongs you.

I know what you are saying, "You don't know they did to me. They hurt me deeply and I need to give them what they deserve." But hold on and wait a minute! You have not been squeaky clean all of your life. Remember for every finger that you are pointing at someone else, you have four more that are pointing at you. Go ahead and tell the truth and say that you are guilty as charged.

Paul quotes from Deuteronomy 32:34 to show that God has always declared His intentions to take vengeance on those who wrong others. What a declaration for justice, for us and those we care about. For everyone that has been wronged, Paul gives a warning, "Vengeance is Mine, said the Lord." Paul wants us to know that we must trust God and God's time table for His vengeance. Remember, His timing is not our timing, but God is always on time. We must trust God at His word and by His power to deliver whatever justice that He sees fit.

God's thoughts are not our thoughts and His ways are not our ways. So now you maybe thinking, maybe God will show that person some mercy? Maybe or maybe not. But God shows us mercy everyday.

God is simple telling us to just trust Him to handle the revenge and the justice to all that harms us, because God says, "Vengeance is mine."

BITTERNESS

Bitterness is a feeling of deep anger and resentment. Bitterness is an emotion which encompasses both anger and hate. Often people who are bitter, go around being angry and ugly to everyone and everything. However, bitterness is often a result of something that happened in their past which hurt them, scarred them, and/or injured them.

Bitterness is a very unattractive character in any person who feels the need to take their emotions out on other people who are usually just innocent and honest. Bitterness is hard to admit or accept and the results end in a lesson of bitterness.

Bitterness is associated with being angry and holding grudges. Hebrews 12:15 states, "See to it that no one fails to obtain the grace of

God; that no 'root of bitterness' springs up and causes trouble, and by it many become defiled?"

What does it mean "root of bitterness?" The seed of bitterness is a hurt that is planted in someone. The hurt may be intentional or unintentional. Sometimes things are taken out or perspective, someone didn't mean to hurt you, but you were hurt. Sometimes the hurt and pain are just imaginary. No one meant to hurt you, but somehow you feel that you have been injured. Sometimes the hurt could be a chastisement from God. " The soil of bitterness is a heart that harbors hostility and does not deal with hurt by the grace of God." When someone becomes bitter, the bitterness takes root in the heart and grows deeper.

There are a lot of bitter people in this world. They have not dealt with their old wounds. They are critical of people. They are always finding fault with people and they will find a way to justify their feelings and their actions.

Bitterness affects you emotionally, spiritually, and physically. Bitterness is a fruit of evilness. It is not of God. Bitterness is a form of hatefulness. Hatefulness and Holiness cannot dwell in the same heart. They CANNOT co-exist.

Some people will have the nerves to say that they know themselves and bitterness is not in their hearts. God knows your heart and He tells us, "The heart is deceitful above all things and desperately wicked: who can know it?"

So how do you cure a bitter heart? First, you need to ask God to forgive you. If you are sincere, He will. Second, ask God to clean your heart. Then, learn to catch yourself whenever those thoughts of bitterness began to attack you. Learn to replace those evil thoughts with good thoughts.

Hebrews 12:14 says, "Follow peace with all men, and holiness, without which no man shall see the Lord."

I know what you are saying, "Look at what they did to me?" Did they really wrong you or was it a misunderstanding and you just perceived that you were wrong? If they wronged you innocently or on purpose, God says, "Beloved never avenge yourselves, but leave it to the wrath of God, for it is written, 'Vengeance is mine, I will repay, says the Lord" (Romans 12:19).

When you forgive someone, you are setting two people free, and one of them is you.

DOING YOUR OWN THING

I know that you have heard the phrase, "Doing Your Own Thing." Young people that are still living at home, have the tendency to pout and say, "I just want to live my own life and do my own thing." I believe that you can do your own thing and live your own life when you start paying your own mortgage or rent.

In the 1960s and 1970s, the Hippies develop a counter-cultural movement that rejected the mores of mainstream American life. The movement originated on college campuses in the United States and spread to other countries. The name Hippy derived from the word "hip". This group began to present us with a subjective behavior, "doing your own thing."

"Doing your own thing" means to do something without help. To fend for yourself. To go solo. To stand alone and stand on your own two feet. To do something of your own accord, even if it means that there is the possibility of sinking.

We can't do anything on our own. God is our Sustainer, Protector, and Provider. When you try to eliminate God out of your life, then you have committed spiritual suicide. You become spiritually bankrupt and your life will be filled with nothing but chaos. You will be in the wilderness and drowning in the quicksands of evilness.

In the Book of Judges, there was a period of total national corruption and confusion. Do this sound like today? "In those days there was no king in Israel: every man did that which was right in his own eyes" Judges 21:25.

The whole picture is very sad. Israel had set aside the principles that were so important to GOD. There was no regard for God. No regard for God's law and no regard for others. They were all about themselves. They were just "doing their own thing." Everybody did as they saw fit in their own eyes. That means, "That Anything Goes."

This is happening to us now? Everybody is doing their "own thing" as if God doesn't exist and He can't see. They are doing their "own thing" in any and every way that they can. They don't care who they step on or who gets hurt.

These are some dark times. We are faced with problems, problems, and more problems. We have problems at home. We have problems on the job. We have problems in the church. There are drug problems and political problems. Everybody wants to be the captain of their own ship. People are all about me, myself, and I. It is all about self and a self-centered lifestyle.

Do you know what the problem is? The problem is a "SPIRITUAL" one. We need to get back to God and our spiritual foundation. That is where we got off track and that is where our problems began. We saw in the Book of Judges what happened when you suffer from spiritual bankruptcy. We are suffering from a very surreal bankruptcy today and it is Spiritual.

We need God! We need God's rules! We need to seek God and worship Him! We need to return to the church and be obedient to the Word of God!

We don't need to be "doing our own thing," but doing the "right thing" in the eyes of God.

Paul has warned us, "Don't copy the behavior and customs of this world but be a new and different person with a fresh newness in all you do and think. Then you will learn from your own experience how his ways will really satisfy you" Romans 12:2.

GOD'S GIFT

How do you feel when you receive a gift? I love giving gifts and I love to receive them as well. Oh, the excitement of it all! It feels really good to receive a gift. It feels equally as good because it let you know that someone thought about you in a kind and generous way.

We as humans want to feel special. We want to be loved. Matter of fact, we crave for that special feeling of being happy and wanted.

Receiving a gift is just another human behavior of feeling special and happy.

Giving a gift must come from the heart. When you give gifts, you are giving something willingly and without wanting something in return.

We give people gifts for a number of reasons and occasions. We give gifts to celebrate a birthday. We give gifts to show appreciation to someone special. We give gifts just to say, "thank you". We give gifts for a promotion, a new job, when someone purchases a new home, to apologize, and because someone passed a test.

No matter what the reason is for giving gifts, the best presents are those that come from the heart.

"Every good and perfect gift is from above, coming down from the Father of the heavenly lights" (James 1:17).

So God gave us the Perfect Gift! What was that? He gave us Jesus Christ! Jesus is the long-awaited Savior, who was prophesied to come in the book of Genesis, when God told the serpent that He would put enmity between it and the seed of the woman. While the serpent would strike His heel (by His crucifixion), ultimately Jesus would crush his head (when He was resurrected).

God loves us. His love is so very deep for us. It is deeper and more profound than we could ever imagine. God's love for us is so great that He sent His only Son to this sinful world to die for our sins. By doing this, God offers us the priceless gift of "eternal life".

Only you can decide (if you have not accepted Jesus) to accept God's gift. Only you can accept God's gift or reject it. Only you can decide to invite Christ into your heart and into your life.

When God's gift is accepted, you will become a child of God, His friend, a member of the Body of Christ, redeemed and forgiven of all your sins. But not just that, you will be an "overcomer" and receive "eternal life."

Let's give thanks to our Lord and Savior for His incomprehensible gift of redemption.

Even while Jesus was hanging on the cross, the people mocked Him, shouting, "He saved others; let him save himself if he is God's Messiah, the Chosen One" (Luke 23:35).

Let's praise God and thank Him that He didn't get off that cross, because what they didn't know, Jesus was saving them and us, when He died upon the cross.

One just needs to accept this precious and mighty special gift from God. The gift of "SALVATION"!

NOT CONNECTED

Have you ever been on your computer or any device that requires Wi-Fi, and suddenly you lose your internet connection? Of course you have! It is just plain outright frustrating, especially when you are working from home, or in the middle of a lesson, or just plain "surfing the web".

Many years ago, I had a deep conversation with a particular person, about God. She was an avid church goer, a member on the Trustee Board, and an Usher. She was also on the Finance Committee and the President on the Pastor's Aid Committee. She loved her pastor and she loved her church.

In my conversation with her, she wanted to know why did I cry often in church. I simply told her that I cried because I felt the presence of the Holy Spirit. She was perplexed at my answer, because

135

she did not know how that felt. She said that she wished she could experience it, but she had never had such an experience. In other words, she was really "not connected" to God.

I remember when I was a young Christian, I thought something was wrong when I didn't feel that feeling (the presence of the Holy Spirit) all of the time. I confronted my late husband about my concern. He just snickered and told me that I was just fine. I wasn't disconnected from God. He informed me that, that feeling does not linger with you all day and all night, but the Spirit of God will always be within me.

I know there maybe times in our lives when we have a feeling of being "not connected" to God. Sometimes, it may feel like we have lost our passion for our pursuit of God. Sometimes the busyness of our life gets us off-track. Sometimes, we just get stuck and get distracted. Sometimes we may have the tendency to put God on pause. Thus, causing us to feel "not connected".

Hebrews 12:1-2, can be used as a guide to help you get reconnected in your spiritual walk. "Therefore we also, since we are surrounded by so great a cloud of witnesses, let us lay aside every weight, and the sin which so easily ensnares us, and let us run with endurance the race that is set before us. Looking unto Jesus, the author and finisher of our faith, who for the joy that was set before Him endured the cross despising the shame, and has sat down at the right hand of the throne of God."

Sometimes we may feel that God has pulled away from us, but this is "ABSOLUTELY INCORRECT". God is always there for us, with us, instructing us, supporting us, and encouraging us. God is our greatest "Cheerleader".

Sometimes we will allow people, places and things to create a space between us and God; thereby, blocking our intimacy with Him. This situation may come in all kinds of forms, such as busyness, careers, people, social media, and even disappointments in life. It can come from anything that distracts our attention from God; even servicing others or your church can be a distraction.

So what do you do? Throughout the Bible, God has said that if we pursue Him, and draw near to Him, then He will draw near to us. Hebrews 12:2 says: focus our eyes on Jesus. It is not merely that we need to spend more time with Him, but talk to Him, pray to Him, worship Him, and talk to fellow Christians that are deeply rooted in Him.

Our relationship with God is truly a personal one. God should always be #1 in our lives, that means that He is our "Top Priority". He is "PRIORITY ONE"!

When we dedicate our hearts and time to Him, that feeling of disconnect will be replaced with a "super connection". So let us be like Clark Kent, go into the telephone booth, regroup and refocus, and when you step out of the booth, you will become "SUPER CHARGED".

"Let us lay aside every weight, and the sin which doth so easily besets us, and let us run with patience the race that is set before us" (Hebrews 12:1).

What is weighing you down? Your path of life! Most of us are hauling too much weight. Too many things to do in one day. Too many entanglements with people. Too many shoulda's, woulda's, and coulda's. Too many worries, guilts, and regrets. Too many physical and mental stuff that you are carrying around. They are complicating your life. They are weighing you down. They are keeping you stuck in neutral.

No one is perfect. We all carry some weight, some more than others. These weights sometimes impede our spiritual growth. Sometimes the weight is sin. Sometimes we do things that we know are wrong, but we are unwilling to let them go. Sin entangles us and trip us up. We get tripped up in our daily Christian walk over bitterness, jealousy, strife, lying, and so on.

Sometimes the weight is besetting sin. Those sins that we have tried to get rid of but they keep coming back, time and time again. They eat away at us like cancer. Like memories of our past mistakes and bad habits that we seem like we just can't break, and many more besetting sins that keeps us from moving forward.

Sometimes the weight is a distraction. Some weights are not sinful, but they keep us from progressing spiritually. The author of Hebrews says, "…laying aside every weight…that so easily ensnares us." There are many things that are not sinful, in and of themselves. They have the potential to become weights that will slow us down, and hold us back. They keep us from moving and running our race. They may be things like ambition, playing cards, surfing the web, and games.

Let's shake off every weight that is weighing us down. Let's run the race that God would be proud of. How do we do this? Paul says, "Forgetting what is behind and reaching forward to what is ahead, I pursue as my goal the prize promised by God's heavenly call in Christ Jesus" (Philippians 3:14).

Whatever demands our attention, to which we are not called by God himself, is to be given as a weight.

God demands that we give our whole attention to his business, to glorify him, to obey his commands, and to promote His interests.

All unnecessary cares, concerns, and burdens are to be considered as a weight.

Laying aside weights and sins is a constant practice. It is not something that happens overnight. It takes time and God will help you every step of the way. Don't get discouraged, or become doubtful. God is always there coaching us on. After all, God is our "Life Coach".

ABBA FATHER

God has so many names and many attributes. We as Christians have heard God referred to as "Abba Father".

God's title of "Abba Father" is only found in the Bible three times, in Romans 8:15, Mark 14:36, and Galatians 4:6, which are all in the New Testament. Only our Lord Jesus, and Apostle Paul have spoken these words, "Abba Father".

"Abba" is the defining term for father in the Aramaic language, spoken by Jesus and Paul as an intimate term to characterize their personal relationship with God.

Paul went from being a Christian hater to a lover of Christ. After encountering Jesus on the road to Damascus, Paul was blinded for three days. His blindness changed his whole perspective about Christ's followers and His faith in God.

Jesus was God in the flesh. When Jesus called God "Abba Father" in the garden of Gethsemane in Mark 14:36, it was a way of acknowledging the power of God.

All of us was created in God's image. As quoted in Genesis 1:27, "So God created man in His own image; in the image of God He created him; male and female He created them."

Knowing this, we as Christians have an unbreakable bond with God. We have a very special relationship with God and an intimacy that cannot be replicated with any other human. The Potter made the clay, that is us, and the making of us, He put time, attention, and love into us.

We are God's children and one of His most significant name is "God our Father". His most cherished attribute is "God is Love". Why? Because He made us. If we owe our birth to our earthly father, how much more do we owe God for creating our whole person and creating it into His own likeness.

God wanted us to look like Himself. Something good and beautiful. An image that is distinct from any other, and yet unmistakably like the Original.

"The Lord is our God; He created us, and we belong to Him; we are his people, the sheep he takes care of in his own pasture" (Psalm 95:7).

If our human parents dotes over us, how much more do you think that our heavenly Father dotes over us?

We belong to God. God loves us and we should love Him back. God cares for us and He takes care of us. God will never forget about us and we should never forget Him. God forgives us and He wants us to forgive others. Because we belongs to Him, He will correct us. He will test us. He will teach us. He will encourage us. He wants us to be perfect. He wants to feel proud of us.

What an absolutely, wonderful, and amazing Father that we have. Thank you "Abba Father"!

THE SITUATION ROOM

In 1961, after the Bay of Pigs, JFK decided he needed a single space to coordinate action during crises. The Situation Room was born. The Situation Room is staffed around the clock in shifts with personnel pulled from the intelligence community. For these permanent staffers, there are three tiny offices and the Watch Floor, the communications center that monitors the world for the National Security Council.

Now that is the description for The Situation Room for the White House of the United States. There is another kind of SitRoom and it is a very important room. What is it you ask? Your Prayer Closet! Jesus has talked about our prayer life on many occasions. Jesus said, "And when you pray, do not be like the hypocrites, for they love to pray standing in the synagogues and on the street corners to be seen by others. Truly I tell you, they have received their reward in full. But when you pray, go into your room, close the door and pray to your Father, who is unseen. Then your Father, who sees what is done in secret, will reward you. And when you pray, do not keep on babbling like pagans, for they think they will be heard because of their many words. Do not be like them, for your Father knows what you need before you ask him" (Matthew 6:5-8).

Some people literally have set aside a room or a quiet place in their home for regular prayer time. That is absolutely wonderful! Your "situation room" or "prayer closet" might be a bench outside, or your kitchen table, or during your daily walk. Jesus usually went to a secluded hillside. The point that I am trying to make is, your "situation room" or "prayer closet" is any place where you can be alone, free from interruptions, distractions, and private.

The perfect "situation room" or "prayer closet," it is a secret place where you can be alone with God to share your deepest thoughts, hurts, feelings, secrets and so on. You can just release everything to him in that secret place. It is just between you and the Lord. It doesn't have to be an actual closet. The point is, that you need to have a spot in your home or apartment where you know that you can be completely alone with God. When you get to that place, you can just talk to him and let it all out. There you can just cry your weeping eyes out. You can be completely honest with God. You can be open, as open as you want to or need to be.

Our "prayer closet" is a place of warfare and peace, struggle and satisfaction. It is a place of patience and action and where sorrow turns into joy and joy into celebration. This place does not have geographical restrictions. This place is not regulated by congress or approved by any executive orders. This place is not reserved for the wealthy or the poor. It is the place of prayer, where you deal with your own situations. This place is your "situation room", thus, your "prayer closet".

Your room, that secret place where you can rest in the shadow of the Almighty. God wants you to be able to come to Him in secret and share your heart with Him You can tell Him any and everything. He is the best confidant! He is always available, 24/7. No matter what you are dealing with, relationship problems, family drama, work, or whatever, you need to know that God is always there for you and that He loves you.

Your "situation room", could be mobile, stationary or both, it doesn't matter. It is when and where you have a special place to talk and listen to God. You can go to your room with expectancy and surrender, hopefulness and acceptance, with a certainty that you will be in God's presence. It is a place of ultimate victory and overwhelming assurance. You don't need an appointment. Walk-Ins are always welcomed. It is your "situation room," this is your "prayer closet". Just walk in! AMEN!

TEARS, RIPS, AND TEARS!

Kintsugi (golden joinery) also known as Kintsukuroi (golden repair), is the Japanese art of repairing broken pottery by mending the areas of breakage with lacquer dusted or mixed with powdered gold, silver, or platinum.

Kintsugi highlights or emphasizes imperfections, visualizing the mends and seam on the broken or cracked piece. The seams on the broken or cracked piece are celebrated, not discarded. The cracks are highlighted with gold, silver, or platinum.

God has created us to be very emotional people. We laugh, we cry, we hurt, we moan, and we groan. There is so much to cry about these days and it may appear so little to rejoice over.

It okay to cry, in fact, we can be comforted knowing that God created us to cry at times. He knows that there will be a time for laughter and a time for crying. Sometimes, our tears can help us release, causing us to feel refreshed and restored. Now that is what I call a "good cry".

Our lives are full of tears, rips, and tears. Things will happen in the lives that rip and tear us apart. The loss of a loved one; the injustices in the world; watching the ever increasing food lines for the needed at different churches; fears and disappointments, just to name a few.

Sometimes things happen to us or others, that will make us feel as though our hearts have been ripped out. There are things that will tear us apart and cause us so much pain that we will shed unbelievable and painful tears. "The eyes of the Lord are on the righteous and his ears are attentive to their cry" Psalm 34:15).

Even when we cry in secret or behind closed doors, God sees our tears. God feels our pain. He knows when we have been wounded. He knows when we are disappointed and when people put us down and let us down. He pities our every moan and groan.

But the Bible clearly tells us that Jesus wept too. Jesus was God, and yet He was a human. He experienced the same emotions that we have. He knows how it feels to be disappointed, to moan, to be lied on, to be brokenhearted, and to be betrayed. He cried when he saw the pain of those He loved, and when He saw the sinful nature of man. He knows how it feels to be torn and ripped apart, and He expressed it sometimes with tears.

One day our pain and hurt will disappear, and we will never cry again. We will never feel the rip and tear that brings about so many tears. God has prepared a place for His children. A place that has not been built by man's hands. There will be no more ripping and tearing. There will be no more sorrow or mourning. There will be peace, joy, and happiness, for all of eternity.

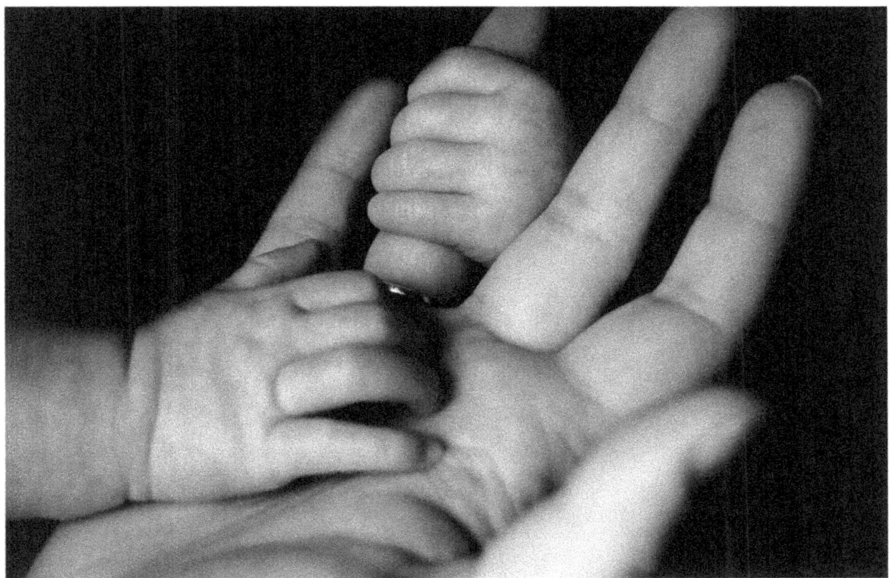

REGRETFULLY YOURS

Everyone has some type of regret. No one can get through life without wishing that you didn't make a bad decision, because of the consequences of that decision. You wished you had stayed in touch with some good friends, who were your best buddies and someone drops dead unexpectedly. Or you regret breaking up with the love of your life or maybe getting dumped by them.

Regretfully is used when you are full or regrets, like when you called in sick from work, and you decide to leave home and go out to get a quick bite, and who do you run into, the job's biggest snitch. BUSTED!

Regretful describes the feeling of being sorry for something that you did or didn't do, or something that happened.

Regret is a feeling of sorrow, wishing you could do something differently or undo an action. So when you are regretful, you might feel frustrated, disappointed with yourself, embarrassed, or even sad.

Paul said, "Even if I caused you sorrow by my letter, I do not regret it. Although I did regret it, I now see that my letter caused you sorrow, but only for a short time. And now I rejoice, not because you were made sorrowful, but because your sorrow led you to repentance. For you felt the sorrow that God had intended, and so were not harmed in any way by us..." (2 Corinthians 7:8-9).

The Bible has much to say about shame and regret, and believe me, there are plenty of examples of people in the Bible who have experienced these feelings.

Can you imagine the shame and regret Adam and Eve must have felt after their sin? They were in the perfect world, in the perfect situation, with the perfect relationship with God.

Can you imagine how Peter felt, the shame and embarrassment and regret, right after the Passover meal? Peter tells Jesus that he would lay down his life for Him. Jesus responds by telling him that on that very night, Peter would not deny Him once, but three times.

Everybody was born with a sin nature, that is the natural inclination to sin. Our God is sovereign, and He had a plan to redeem us, through His Son, Jesus Christ. God gave us a choice for salvation and eternal life with Him.

The Bible teaches us that, when we confess our sins and have faith in Christ, we become His children. We are cleanse from all of our unrighteousness. We can cast our sins on Him and they will be removed as far as the east is from the west.

Yes, some of us regret our mistakes, but we don't have to beat ourselves up about them. For those of us who can't move forward and is living in the past, maybe you can find comfort in Romans 8:1, "There is now no condemnation for those who are in Christ Jesus."

We are sinners, but we are justified by faith. We may have a shameful past, but we have a better glorious future. We used to walk in foolishness, but now we walk in Christ.

God has forgiven us of those things, and sins that we feel ashamed of and regret. Now we can stop dictating that imaginary letter in our heads, with the closing valediction of, "Regretfully Yours".

HUNGRY

Hunger and thirst are frequent human urges. It is extremely satisfying to eat a meal when you are hungry or to drink water when you are thirsty.

What does being hungry do to your body? The body's system is very complex. "Hunger hormones" (ghrelin) in your blood, and an empty stomach signal the brain when you are hungry. Nerves in the stomach send signals to the brain that you are full.

What does spiritual hunger mean? Just as your stomach growls for food, your spirit longs for God.

"I am the bread of life. Whoever comes to me will never be hungry, and whoever believes in me will never be thirsty" (John 6:35).

Our bodies were designed to require nourishment, so it is normal to feel hungry when it is time to eat. It works the same way with our spirit. We were created to fellowship and worship God.

God has a banquet prepared for us. It is the perfect feast of His presence. We were made for God and for His purpose. To honor Him, to glorify Him, and to pursue Him.

Psalm 34:8 says, "taste and see that the Lord is good." But what does "taste" mean in the Spirit? When we "taste" food, we put it in our mouths, to experience its flavor, its texture, and its composition. In the Spirit, "tasting" means to experience the nature of God. What a very pleasant delicious meal, because every "taste" makes you want more and more of God.

When we are aware of God's presence in our lives, He makes Himself known to us. It could be in a "still small voice", like a whisper; through visions or dreams; sometimes a sweet fragrant smell; or being slain in the Spirit. Whatever your experience, you will know that you have tasted God and that special encounter will have you begging for more.

How do we "taste"? In the natural, we sit down at the table and eat by putting food in our mouths. In the spirit, we get to know God through prayer, talking to Him, in worship, reading and studying His holy Word, the Bible, and practice feeling His presence.

Are you hungry? Then pursue God! Sit down at His banquet table every chance that you get. Eat the food that He has prepared for you. Feast on God! Come "taste" and see that God is good!

SELF-MADE

I have heard people say on several occasions that: "He is a self-made man" or "She is a self-made woman."

Forbes defines "self-made" as someone who built a company or established a fortune on his or her own, rather than inheriting some or all of it.

I love to hear and read stories of how people climbed from "rags to riches" and how they overcame adversity against all odds. So many of us have the potential, but some have not walked into their purpose, for some reason or another.

I have a problem with people thinking that they did it all my themselves, because we can't do nothing without God, through Jesus Christ. We are absolutely nothing without Him.

We were not made from our own creation. That means that we can't be self-made. When it comes to God, we are not self-supporting, self-sustaining, self-sufficient, nor self-dependent.

In Paul's first letter to Timothy, he gives a warning that is relevant still today, Paul says, "Command those who are rich in this present age not to be haughty, nor to trust in uncertain riches but in the living God, who gives us richly all things to enjoy" - 1 Timothy 6:17.

It is not a sin to have material wealth, it is the high-mindedness that Jesus is concern with. The Bible warns us about this through other related words, such as, haughtiness, arrogance, and pride.

To be proud means to be high in the wrong sense. It means to have an arrogant and exaggerated view of yourself and your abilities. One word for pride comes from the Greek word meaning, "envelope with smoke" or to be "puffed-up". "High minded, puffed-up, and blowing smoke," you get the picture.

God hates haughtiness and pride! Pride is the nature of God's enemy and our enemy, the devil. Haughtiness, arrogance, and pride of life are the sins, which led Satan to try to attempt to exalt himself above God, and to rule God's kingdom. "For thou hast said in thine heart, I will ascend into heaven, I will exalt my throne above the stars of God: I will sit also upon the mount of the congregation, in the sides of the north: I will ascend above the heights of the clouds; I will be like the most High" Isaiah 14:13-14.

None of us are self-made in the true sense, but we are all God made. All success comes from God. No one got to be successful all by themselves. Everyone owes someone something, be it your parents, a friend, spouse, teacher, and the list goes on and on.

Whatever success comes our way, we should always take the time to thank God, after all, God allowed it to happen, and God deserves ALL of the credit.

EVERYTHING

Everything, everyone, everybody, and everywhere are indefinite pronouns. We use them to refer to a total number of people, places and things.

"Be anxious for nothing, but in everything by prayer and supplication, with thanksgiving, let your requests be made known to God" (Philippians 4:6).

Imagine having to worry about anything and everything. To worry about everything seems like the impossible. Or is it? I am one that worries about everything. I am the "worrier," tagged by my mother.

I don't think anything has really changed about me, except, I have learned to give my worries and concerns to God.

"Be anxious for nothing," or maybe not be overly anxious. Worry about nothing; pray about everything. Prayer is the secret weapon of power.

"Worry about nothing." In Philippians 4:4, we were given one of the new commandments that God give us: Worry about nothing; pray about everything. Nothing is nothing, and we are to worry about nothing. Our bills are real. Our sickness is real. Our problems are real. So how are we to worry about nothing? Are we supposed to ignore these things that are real? No! Paul says, we are to worry about nothing, but PRAY about everything.

Pray about EVERYTHING! Pray about the big things and the little things and the tiniest things. Yes, even those trifling things. EVERYTHING!

That means, we must pray without ceasing. That means, that we should be living in holy communion with our Holy Father, through Jesus, all day long. And even when we wake-up in the middle of the night, we still should be talking to God. Taking EVERYTHING, to God in prayer.

It should be a spiritual instinct, again and again, bringing our various matters to Him. Whatever is bothering us, in any way, just tell our Holy Father. Speak to Him, He is just waiting for you to pour your heart out to Him.

Apostle Paul says that we should turn our worries into prayers. Whenever you start to worry, just stop and pray. Tell God your needs, then thank Him for the answer.

Let your prayer rest on your faith and your faith rests on the Word of God. Take it to God, then thank Him and leave it there with Him.

Thank Him for His answer to your prayer. However and whatever ways He wish to answer your prayer. Talk to Him! Take it to Him! Leave it with Him! And, thank him. AMEN!

HELLO MY CHILD,

I am appreciative that you always take time to talk to me. You are most thankful for all of the blessings that I have bestowed upon you. You always take the time to thank me for your seen and unseen blessings. You are always thankful for your going out and coming in. You are always grateful to me for waking you up everyday. You are thankful for My protection of you during the day, and for your lying down at night. You show gratitude for everything that I have given you. You never began eating your food until you bless it. You are thoughtful, considerate, humble, kind hearted, sympathetic, caring, generous, and attentive to others.

You pour your heart out to me daily. You spare absolutely nothing. You understand that I know everything about you. I know what you are concern about, and the things that troubles you. The things you love and the things that you dislike. I know when you are happy and when you are sad.

So answer this question for me, if you tell me that you are going to let me handle your problems, why do you keep taking them back, once you finished your prayers?

You are supposed to cast all of your cares on me. You always talk to me and you are sincere. But those things that worry you, those things that burdens you, those things that are weighing you down, you are still trying to handle them, yourself. Those things puts you in bondage. They are chains that bonds you and they have you shackled.

I can provide you relief from any bondage that you carry. You don't need to fear nor feel trapped, nor believe that you have failed. You see, it is written, "come unto me, all ye that labour and heavy laden, and I will give you rest. Take my yoke upon you, and learn of me; I am meek and lowly in heart: and ye shall find rest unto your souls. For my yoke is easy, and my burden is light" (Matthew 11:28-30).

This is one of your favorite scriptures and you recite it often. Especially when you are worried, but you are not applying it to your situations.

Let me approach you in a different way. You love baseball, right? Let's say that the baseball is your worry, your problem. And let's say that I am the baseball bat. Now give me that ball (your problem), and watch Me hit that ball right out of the park (your life). WOW! Another home run for Team Jesus.

WINNING! All because you Let Go and Let God.

Your Loving GOD!

www.ingramcontent.com/pod-product-compliance
Lightning Source LLC
Chambersburg PA
CBHW051118300726

48981CB00002B/179